From Anna

from Anna

JEAN LITTLE
Illustrated by Joan Sandin

HarperTrophy
A Division of HarperCollinsPublishers

CONTENTS

For Anne
with my love

This story begins in Germany in the year 1933, a time in that country's history when many of its citizens were being denied personal freedoms and it was dangerous for anyone to speak out against such injustice. Some Germans, like Anna's father, became so worried about the future they took their families and moved to a new world.

1 • A SONG FOR HERR KEPPLER

Let it really be Papa, Anna wished desperately as she tugged open the big front door. Let me be right.

She wanted to run down the steps but they were uneven and she had fallen headlong down them before now. That was no way to meet Papa, landing at his feet upside down and with a fresh batch of bruises. The moment she was on flat ground, however, she ran. Then she was close enough to be sure—and she *was* right.

"Papa, Papa!" she cried in delight, flinging her arms around his middle and hugging him. The next instant she was trying to get away. She, Anna, never grabbed

people like that, not right out on the street where anyone could see. But Papa had dropped his briefcase and
was hugging her back so hard you could tell he would
not mind if all the world were watching.

"Stop, stop! You're breaking my bones," Anna
gasped at last.

Laughing, he let go of her. At once she became very
busy picking up the briefcase, dusting it off with part
of her skirt and giving it back to him. She kept her
head bent so he would not catch her joy at being the
first to meet him, at the wonderful hug, at everything.
But Papa guessed. He reached down and captured one
of her hands and swung it in his as they started for the
house.

"Where are the others?" he asked.

Anna scowled. Why were the older four always so
important? And yet of course he would wonder. She
could not remember ever before having been the only
one to meet him. Always Gretchen or Rudi, Fritz or
Frieda, or even all four, had been there too.

"They're busy fighting about what happened in
school today," she explained. "But I sat on the window-
sill and watched until I saw you coming."

She was dragging her feet now. She so wanted him
to herself a few moments longer.

"What happened in school?" he asked. He let go
of her hand, and they both stopped walking while he
waited to hear. Without thinking about it, Anna
reached up and jerked on one of her thin braids. It
was a habit she had when she was worried.

"Don't, Anna," Papa warned. "It'll come undone."

He was too late. Anna looked down in dismay at the crumpled ribbon in her fist. So often Mama begged her to leave her hair alone. So often she forgot.

"Maybe I can fix it," Papa said. "I can try anyway."

Anna turned her back and held the ribbon up over her shoulder to him. Awkwardly he bundled together the loose hair into one strand. Her mother was right about it being difficult. Wisps of it kept slipping away from him. But at last, while Anna clutched the end, he tied a lopsided bow around the middle. He frowned at it. He had made no attempt to rebraid it and it looked all wrong. Anna knew how it looked as well as he did, but she told herself she did not care. Even when it was newly done by Mama herself, it never looked just right, like Gretchen's smooth, gleaming thick braids.

"About school, Papa," she reminded him, turning around.

Papa forgot her hair too.

"What happened?"

For one instant, Anna hesitated. It was really Gretchen's story, not hers. But Gretchen and the rest so often had something to tell. There was never anything she, Anna, could say about her troubled days in Frau Schmidt's class. Anyway, it was Gretchen's own fault she hadn't been watching out for Papa!

"We were all at Assembly," Anna plunged in. "We always have Assembly before we start classes and we sing then. We get to choose a couple of the songs. The older children, that is. This morning it was Gretchen's turn and she asked for 'Die Gedanken sind frei.' The whole school knows it except for the younger children. I'm the only one in my class who knows it all."

Anna paused, proud of her knowledge and remembering the day Papa had taught her the song, when she was only five years old. He had explained the proud words until she understood them and then they had marched along together, singing it. *Die Gedanken sind frei.* It meant "thoughts are free."

"So what happened?" Papa said again.

"Well, Herr Keppler . . . You know, Papa, he's the new Headmaster the government sent after Herr Jakobsohn left."

Papa nodded, and his face darkened. He and Herr Jakobsohn had been friends. They had played chess together. But the Jakobsohns had gone to America three weeks ago.

"Herr Keppler just said, 'We will not sing that song in this school again.' Fräulein Braun had already started to play the beginning to get us started and nobody knew what to do. Gretchen was still standing up and she went all red and said right out loud, 'Why?' That was brave of her, Papa. Everybody is frightened of Herr Keppler. When Rudi says he isn't, he's lying."

"What answer did Herr Keppler give Gretchen?" Papa said.

He sounded angry, almost as though he already knew.

"He didn't answer her at all," Anna said. She was

4

still surprised as she thought back. "I mean, he didn't give any reason. He just looked at her and said, 'Sit down.' " The command came sharply from Anna's lips as she imitated the Headmaster.

"Rudi says maybe Herr Keppler just doesn't like that song and that it didn't mean anything special. . . ." Her voice trailed off uncertainly.

"What did you sing instead?" Papa asked, beginning, once again, to move slowly toward the house. As they walked, he looked not at her but at the ground.

" 'Deutschland, Deutschland über alles.' "

They were at the steps now. Their time alone was almost over. Anna's shoulders drooped.

Then all at once, Papa threw back his head, stood still, and started to sing.

> Die Gedanken sind frei,
> *My thoughts freely flower.*
> Die Gedanken sind frei,
> *My thoughts give me power.*
> *No scholar can map them.*
> *No hunter can trap them.*
> *No man can deny*
> Die Gedanken sind frei.

How could Herr Keppler not like words like that? Or the tune, either? It rang out in the quiet street. Anna joined in the second verse. She sang with all her might, just the way Papa did, as if every phrase mattered.

So I think as I please
And this gives me pleasure;
My conscience decrees
This right I must treasure;

At that, Anna heard them coming—Rudi leaping down the stairs two at a time, Gretchen hurrying after him, the twins tumbling behind the older two. The door burst open. The four of them looked at their sister and their father. Then, all together, they were singing too.

My thoughts will not cater
To duke or dictator,
My thoughts freely fly.
Die Gedanken sind frei.

"Papa, did Anna tell you . . . ?" Gretchen cut in. But Papa was leading the way in, still singing. They followed him as though he were the Pied Piper of Hamelin town, and all of them joined in the wonderful last verse.

And if tyrants take me
And throw me in prison,
My thoughts will burst free,
Like blossoms in season.
Foundations will crumble.
The structure will tumble.
And free men will cry,
"Die Gedanken sind frei!"

They finished the song in the downstairs hall. Mama put her head over the stairwell and glared down at them.

"Ernst, have you lost your mind?" she demanded. "Little Trudi Grossman had been sick all day and Minna has just got her to sleep. What were you thinking of anyway, making such a racket?"

They had climbed up to her by that time. Papa caught her around the waist and kissed her so that she blushed. He was laughing now, though sorry too about perhaps disturbing the baby. But no wakening wail came from the downstairs apartment, so maybe that was all right.

"One last fling, Klara," he told her. "One song for Herr Keppler, who cannot keep me from singing with my own children yet."

"What nonsense!" Mama scoffed, freeing herself.

"Anna did tell you!" Gretchen cried.

Anna looked at her feet. But she was still glad she had been the one to let Papa know all about it.

"Yes. Anna told me." Papa's voice was heavy and tired suddenly. The fun was over.

"But it doesn't mean anything, Papa, does it?" Rudi asked. Earlier he had been certain, but now he sounded shaken.

"I tell you it does." Gretchen, usually so calm, was near tears. "It wasn't just the way he spoke to me. You should have seen the look he gave Fräulein Braun. Her hands started to shake. I saw. I thought she wasn't going to be able to play our national anthem."

"And I keep trying and trying to tell you all that that's not the worst thing that happened today," Fritz burst out. "Well, I guess it didn't happen today exactly—but Max Hoffman's father has disappeared! Vanished! He's been gone for three days."

He waited for them to gasp at this news. To Fritz, it was exciting but not real. He had not spoken to Max himself. Another boy had told him. Anna, though, had talked to Gerda, Max's sister. She stood there remembering Gerda's face, swollen from crying.

"Which Hoffmans are you talking about?" Mama said, on her way back to the stove. "Nobody we know would do a thing like that to his family. It's a disgrace."

"But he didn't . . ." Anna started, forgetting, this once, that she was the youngest, remembering only Gerda's wounded eyes. "I mean, it wasn't like that. Gerda told me."

"Oh, Anna Solden, look at your hair!" Mama interrupted.

Her mind still on Gerda, Anna paid no attention. She had to make them see, make them understand. Then maybe Papa could help somehow.

"The Hoffmans had supper waiting. On the table even. And they waited and waited and Herr Hoffman just didn't come. And when Frau Hoffman went to the police, they would hardly even listen, Gerda said. They told her to go on home and keep quiet about it."

Papa was really listening to her. He looked as

troubled as she felt. But Mama laughed.

"The police know these things happen," she said. "I don't suppose she's the first wife that's gone to them looking for a runaway husband. But really, what could have happened to him? He could come home if he wanted to—unless he had an accident or a heart attack or something. I suppose she checked the hospitals?"

"I guess so," Anna mumbled.

She knew so little, really.

"He has been gone three days," she added.

"I already said that," Fritz said.

"It's no accident then," Mama dismissed the whole thing. She put down the steaming dish she was holding.

"Come on now. Forget Herr Hoffman while the food is good and hot," she told her family. "He's probably having a fine supper himself somewhere. Leave that bow alone, Anna. I'll fix it later."

Papa sat down in his big chair. The others took their places. All heads were bowed for the blessing. Then, just when they thought their father had finished, he added, "And, dear Father God, have mercy on the Hoffman family tonight and on this troubled country and . . . on all children, in Jesus' name, Amen."

They raised their heads and stared at him.

Mama was the one to speak.

"Ernst, what is this that you are talking about? There have been many people out of work, it is true, and everything has been expensive. But the troubled times are ending. Everyone knows that."

Anna looked at her father. He would know. He would set her fears at rest at last. What must it be like to sit at the window and watch for Papa and never see him come? The thought had haunted her all day. Papa picked up his fork slowly.

"The troubled times . . ." he said. "I think they are just beginning. We are seeing only a faint shadow of the darkness that threatens us."

"Ernst!" Mama cried, horrified at his words and the sorrow in his face and understanding little more than Anna did.

"Never mind now, Klara," Papa said. "This is not the time to talk."

But Anna was shaken to the core. Her father was afraid. He could not comfort her after all. And she had not even told him everything.

"Frau Hoffman wanted Gerda to ask Herr Keppler for help," she said now. "But Max wouldn't go to him and Gerda doesn't want to either. Papa, what should they do?"

"Herr Keppler will not help," Papa said, the same darkness in his voice that she had seen on his face earlier. Then he smiled at her. It was a smile of love, but with no hope in it.

"I will go and talk to Frau Hoffman and see if I can do anything," he promised.

He was still afraid though. Anna did not know how she knew. Maybe because she was so often frightened herself. If only she could comfort him somehow!

She took a mouthful while she thought hard. Then an idea came. She was not sure whether it was a good idea or not. Papa was eating now too. She reached out quietly and touched his hand so that he looked at her again. She did not want the others to hear. They might laugh. Rudi often said she was crazy.

But Mama's cabbage rolls were too good to keep waiting, no matter how serious life might be. Nobody was paying any attention to her except her father.

" 'Thoughts are free,' Papa," Anna said softly.

Papa's head came up. He smiled right at her, a real smile this time, and cupped his large hand around her small one, giving it a good warm squeeze.

"No matter what I have to do, I'll keep it that way for you, my Anna," he promised her.

Anna did not know what he meant. What could he have to do? Did he mean talking to Frau Hoffman? Or something else?

She could not answer herself but she did know that she had said the right thing. Not Rudi or Gretchen or Fritz or Frieda, but she, Anna! Happily, she took another bite.

2 • THE TROUBLED TIMES

"Are you going to Gerda's tonight, Papa?" Anna asked.

"Not tonight," Papa told her. He looked troubled. "Tomorrow night I will go, *Liebling*. Maybe by then everything will be all right."

Anna knew he was saying that because she was a child. Papa himself did not believe things were going to be all right. Anna prayed he was wrong.

The next morning Gerda was at school but she did not speak to anyone. Anna stood near her when she could do it without being too obvious. She almost said, more than once, "Don't worry, Gerda. My father is coming to your house tonight. He will find some way to fix things. He will find out where your father is."

But she remembered the look on Papa's face, as though he knew more than he was saying. She did not want Gerda to hope if there really was no hope.

Gerda did not seem to see Anna hovering close to her. All day long her face looked as if it were behind shutters.

"Pay attention, Gerda," Frau Schmidt snapped.

There was a second's silence. Then Gerda's voice said mechanically, "Yes, Frau Schmidt."

That night, as soon as the Soldens were finished eating, Papa went over to the Hoffman house.

"Maybe it is dangerous, Ernst," Mama said, just as he was leaving.

"Maybe I can help," he said and went.

He was home much too soon. When he opened the door, Anna whirled around, hoping, hoping that she would see in his face that Herr Hoffman had come home safely.

"They've left Frankfurt," he said instead. "If only I had gone earlier . . . but I don't suppose it would have made any difference."

The next day in school, Anna Solden sat still listening to the buzz of rumors.

"Herr Hoffman took all their money with him."

"They went to her aunt in Rotterdam."

"I heard they went to Berlin."

"You're both crazy. Johann Mitter told me himself that they'd gone to England."

There was a subdued outburst of laughter at that. Johann could always be counted on for a wild story.

"He's lying, same as always," Else Kronen scoffed. "My big brother was talking to the Hoffmans' neighbors and Frau Hoffman left a letter with them to give to Herr Hoffman if he shows up there looking for them. She wouldn't even tell the neighbors where they were going. But you know how Gerda talked about that farm in Austria where they used to go in the summers. . . ."

I'm not saying anything, Gerda, Anna thought. I'm still your friend.

She sat very still waiting for the Assembly. It had been so wonderful to have Gerda single her out to confide in. Of course, there had been nobody else there at first and maybe Gerda had felt safe talking to her because nobody else did. Not often anyway. She was too stupid.

It had started on the very first day, long ago now, when Anna had begun her struggle with the alphabet. To her, many of the letters looked the same. If the letters had stayed still on the page it might have been easier to tell them apart, but when Anna peered at them, they jiggled. She hoped someone else would say something about this. But nobody did, and Anna was afraid to mention it herself. So she held the book closer and closer, trying to make the letters behave.

Then Frau Schmidt had called her to the front to take her turn reciting what she had learned. The teacher used a pointer to spear letters on the blackboard.

"What is this, Anna?" she asked.

Anna did not know. She could not even see it clearly. She stood tongue-tied with shame and didn't make a sound.

"Aren't you Anna Solden?" the teacher asked.

Anna nodded, still unable to speak.

"The sister of Rudolf and Gretchen and the twins?"

Anna nodded again. Her cheeks burned.

"Stand up straight, child, and answer properly. You should say, 'Yes, Frau Schmidt.' "

Somehow Anna straightened.

"Yes, Frau Schmidt," she whispered.

The teacher clicked her tongue against her teeth impatiently.

"Not in a mumble. Speak out," she commanded.

She waited. Anna was trembling by that time. She wondered if she might be going to fall down in front of the whole class. She did not fall.

"Yes, Frau Schmidt," she repeated, praying it was all right.

"Again," rapped out the teacher.

"Yes, Frau Schmidt," Anna said.

"Now let me see if you can name this letter yet," Frau Schmidt said.

Anna could not name the letter. She guessed desperately but her guesses were wrong.

"Oh, go and sit down," the teacher said at last. She watched Anna stumble back to her desk. Then she added mockingly, "I understand your father is an English master in one of the exclusive schools. Perhaps he can teach you something!"

The class laughed. Perhaps they were afraid not to, but Anna did not think of that. She still remembered their laughter.

That had been over a year before. Anna had not yet learned to read. Papa did try to help but he taught English to high-school boys. He could not figure out what was wrong between Anna and the alphabet. But if she could not read, she now could stand up straight. She no longer trembled. She stood stiffly, answered clearly, and hated Frau Schmidt with her whole heart.

And she hated reading too. She did not care that she could not do it. She did not *want* to do it. Why should she? Papa would read to her and Papa loved her just the same, whether she could read or not. She would never read and she would never be friends with the children who laughed at her.

Still, deep inside, it did hurt her that Gerda had not even said good-bye. She had ached so for Gerda in her aloneness and fear. And not once did she, Anna, join in the cruel gossip about where Herr Hoffman might be.

"He's run away with an actress, Johann Mitter says," was one of the stories.

Anna spoke right out against that one.

"He did not," she said.

The others pelted questions at her, really seeing her for once.

"How do you know?"

"Where is he then?"

"Who told you?"

Anna stared back at them defiantly but silently. She had no proof. She just knew. Gerda's father wouldn't.

"Oh, she doesn't know anything," Olga Müller dismissed her. "As usual," she added.

They turned away in disgust.

But Anna was sure she was right. Something must have gone terribly wrong to keep Herr Hoffman from coming home. It was part of the "troubled times" Papa had spoken about.

"Anna, you cannot afford to sit and dream," Frau Schmidt snapped. "Not if you want to finish the Primer."

"Yes, Frau Schmidt," she said automatically.

She opened the book she could not read and prepared for another day at school.

A week later, she wakened in the night to hear Mama shouting.

"Leave Germany! Ernst! How *could* we?"

Papa's voice rumbled some reply. Anna shook her head, still foggy with sleep, and listened harder.

"But this is our *home*!" Mama was more upset than Anna had ever heard her. "We've lived here all our lives. Ernst, I was born not three blocks from this very house. Our friends are here. What about your sister?"

Papa spoke again but though Anna strained her ears, she could only catch occasional words and phrases.

". . . must be brave . . . think of the Hoffmans . . . can't you understand . . ."

He said something about June too. Anna remembered how angry he had been then over some new law. Something about Jews not working for the government . . . Oh, she couldn't remember although she could see him pacing up and down, his eyes flashing. She had not known he could get that angry.

Mama was still arguing.

"But where would we go? Ernst, you are not thinking. What of the children's schooling? Your darling Anna is failing now."

The listening child smiled in the darkness. What if she were failing? Even Mama knew she was Papa's "darling Anna."

"What will happen to her if she is uprooted? And Rudi will probably be Head Boy next term. Anyway we don't have enough money."

At last Papa's voice came strongly through the wall.

"I know all this as well as you do, Klara. But I know much more. Don't you understand that if I were not working in a private school, I would be out of work right now? How long will the new regime overlook the staff at private schools? Remember that Tania's husband is Jewish."

18

"But what does your sister's husband have to do with us?" Beneath her anger, Mama sounded bewildered.

"Oh, Klara, think. Think of the Hoffmans. What happened to him I don't dare guess. Think of Nathan Jakobsohn. Think of the Wechslers. And I heard today that Aaron Singer has been dismissed."

"Ernst, that can't be true. Dr. Singer made that company famous."

"Everyone knows that. But he was dismissed nevertheless. No reasons given. He is going to try to get out of Germany. Soon, I am certain, it will be harder to leave. It is not just the Jews who are in danger, Klara. Anyone who disagrees, anyone who speaks up too loudly . . ."

There was a tense silence. Anna chewed on her fist.

"But your brother Karl is your only relative not in Germany—and he's in Canada!" Mama wailed.

Anna knew that to Mama, Canada was faraway and foreign. Mama had no use for anything "foreign."

Papa yawned suddenly, so widely Anna heard his jaws crack.

"Enough. I'm tired out, Klara. But we must think. If anything happens, we will need to be ready. I wish to God I were wrong about the whole thing."

"I am sure you are wrong," Mama said.

Anna heard her turn over. The bed squeaked. Then Papa added, so softly that Anna nearly missed it, "I made a promise to Anna which I must keep."

"Made what promise to Anna? That you would take us all away from our home?"

"No, not that," Papa said wearily.

Anna had her ear against the wall now, so that she could hear even though his voice dropped.

"I told her she would grow up where thoughts are free," he said.

Had he promised her that? Oh, yes. The song Herr Keppler would not sing. But Mama was storming again.

"So we must all change our lives for your Anna! Why, she is the one of all the children who most needs to stay right here. She is only beginning to learn now. Frau Schmidt says she is stubborn . . . but whatever is wrong, making her start all over again in a new place would be the worst thing in the world for her!"

Anna shuddered. This time, Mama was right. Frau Schmidt was terrible, but some stranger . . . !

Please, Papa, she begged him silently, let us stay here.

Then, incredibly, Klara Solden laughed, an everyday, teasing, comfortable laugh.

"Ernst, you have forgotten how unimportant we are," she said, making nonsense out of all they had been saying. "Why, what could happen to us? Maybe Herr Hoffman's wife was a nag. Maybe Dr. Singer presumed somehow or is getting too old. But we are nobody. Oh, my feet are cold. Put yours over here."

"Klara, Klara," Papa moaned, but his voice had a

faint note of laughter in it too, "you are impossible."

Their voices sank to a murmur. Anna slid back down in bed not knowing whether to worry or not. At last she drifted back into sleep.

She wakened once before morning. There was no sound from her parents' room. For an instant, she was frightened all over again. Then she thought of Mama's cold feet and smiled as she curled up snugly under her own warm covers.

Mama won't let Papa do anything terrible, she thought.

At breakfast everything was the way it had always been. Anna was relieved, though somehow slightly disappointed too. Then at supper Papa made an announcement. It was nothing Anna had expected. But it was terrible enough.

"This family is going to learn to speak English," he said.

His wife and children stared at him. He smiled in return but there was something in that smile which nobody liked.

"We will start right now," he went on, proving their worst fears correct. "From now on, every night, we will speak nothing but English at our evening meal. All of you children, except Anna, have studied some English at school, so you have made a start already," he encouraged them.

"I know no English," Mama said, her face hard.

"You will learn, Klara," Papa said quietly. "We will

begin right now. Listen carefully. Rudi, will you pass me the salt, please?"

The English words sounded like gibberish to Anna. Rudi looked at the pepper, the salt, the mustard. His hand went out slowly. It hovered. Then, uncertainly, it dropped. Luck was with him. He did hand his father the salt.

"Thank you, son," Papa said, taking it.

Rudi's worried look vanished instantly. He glanced around at the others to be sure they had not missed his cleverness. Everyone looked suitably impressed.

But Papa had only started.

"How was school today, Gretchen?" he wanted to know.

Any other time it would have been fun to watch Gretchen get so flustered.

"How . . . how . . . I know not," she stammered.

"It was good, Papa," Rudi put in quickly, brilliantly.

But Gretchen had recovered. She shot her brother a nasty look.

"School was fine, Papa," she said.

Was one right and the other wrong? Anna did not have any idea. It would be wonderful if Rudi had made a mistake already. But suppose Papa turned on her, Anna, next?

This is one million times worse than that alphabet, Anna thought dismally. She tried to sit lower in her chair so that Papa would not see her.

For him it was easy, of course. He actually loved English. He had gone to college in a place called Cambridge. Anna had seen pictures of the river there, of great leaning trees and of young men laughing into the camera. Papa had lots of English books and he read them for fun. He even got English magazines in the mail and he taught English all day long to the boys at Saint Sebastian's.

With a little practice, Rudi and Gretchen did surprisingly well. But it wasn't all just due to their brilliance, as Rudi claimed. He had been learning English in school for four years now and Gretchen for three. The twins had only had one year of it and they made hundreds of mistakes. Mama and Anna were the only two who knew nothing at all about it.

At first they got away with speaking German to each other in spite of Papa. In those days, there was a closeness between them which Anna had not known since she was a baby. She knew that then Mama had cuddled her and had sung to her. There were pictures of her on Mama's knee and Mama's smile at her was beautiful. Anna loved those pictures. But she could not remember, or only barely, a time when she was not a disappointment to her mother.

Even before she had gone off to school, it had started. Anna couldn't run without tripping over some bump in the uneven pavement. Anna could not skip. Anna never could catch a ball unless it was rolled along the ground to her. She *could* learn poems. Papa loved to hear her recite them. But Mama had no time for poems. She wanted a daughter who could at least dust furniture properly.

"Anna, look at all that dust!" she would cry when Anna thought she had finished.

Anna would look and, although she saw no dust at all, she would lower her head in shame.

But now things were different. The two of them would sit and listen to Frieda working so hard to say, "Thank you."

"Tank you, Papa," she would say.

"Put your tongue between your teeth, Frieda, like this. Watch me. *Th . . . th . . . ,*" Papa would demonstrate.

Even Rudi had trouble with the "th" sound.

Then, right in the middle, Anna would whisper to her mother that she wanted more milk. She whispered in German, of course, and Mama answered *"Ja, ja, Liebling,"* and passed it at once. Papa would frown but Anna would sip her milk and feel special and she hardly even cared, much as she loved him.

"My one German child," Mama said fondly on those first evenings. And Anna basked in the sunshine of Mama's smile while it lasted.

Soon enough, she knew, Mama would want to teach her to knit again. Or to sew! That was worse. Gretchen and Frieda were so quick. But Anna simply could not see what Mama meant. She did not understand how, to start with, Mama got the thread through the needle.

When Anna looked at the thin needle in her hand, there was no hole there waiting.

More than once she had almost told Mama that. But always, the next instant, Mama had slid the thread through and was looking at her youngest child with such exasperation that Anna did not know how to explain.

In Mama's needle, there was a hole every time.

Maybe if she held the material closer . . .

"No, no, child," Mama said, "you'll strain your eyes that way. Hold it like this in your lap."

Again her mother sounded so sure. Anna struggled on and got nowhere. Before long, they all grew used to her even though they never stopped trying to improve her.

"Let me, Anna," Gretchen would sigh, taking the potholder from her. "How can you make such huge crooked stitches?"

"Here, Anna. I'll fix it. Really, I cannot understand you. I was knitting socks for my brothers when I was seven."

That was Mama. Gloom closed over Anna. She shut her mouth tight and did not let her hands shake. It was like school and that alphabet. But she would not care. She was Papa's pet even if she wasn't Mama's. Everyone knew that, just as they knew that Mama loved Rudi best, however she denied it.

But now, for a while at least, Anna was Mama's one German child. Oh, Mama still frowned and shook her head over her often but she sang her German songs too, and both of them pretended there were no such things as troubled times.

Anna fought not to remember Gerda, not to wonder where she was and whether her father had ever found them.

She did not waken again to hear her parents quarreling.

It was a good winter, a lovely spring. She took it for granted that the storm had blown over, that eventually Papa would even forget about the English lessons.

Then one morning early in June, 1934, a letter came from Canada. It was not from Uncle Karl; it was from his lawyer.

And overnight, Anna's sometimes happy, often unhappy, but always familiar world turned upside down.

3 • AWKWARD ANNA

That morning on her way to breakfast, Anna met Papa in the hall.

"What is wrong, little one?" Papa asked, seeing her scowl.

Nothing new or different was wrong. It was just that Anna was feeling ugly. She always felt ugly by the time Mama had finished straining and twisting her hair back into the two tight skimpy braids. She had to sit to have this done, right in front of her mother's mirror, and she could not miss seeing herself.

The rest of the family were so beautiful. Gretchen and Rudi were tall and fair like Papa. Their hair did

not just shine; it was also well behaved. Their eyes were bright blue. Their cheeks were pink. Not too pink, but not just plain no-color like Anna's own. Fritz and Frieda were Mama over again with their black curls, their sparkling brown eyes and their lively impish faces.

Then there was Anna, her forehead knobbly, her hair wispy and dull, her eyes blue but grayish and small. Her ears and her nose were fine but there was nothing special about them. And her mouth looked . . .

"Stubborn," Mama would have said, or "sulky."

"Unhappy," Papa would have said.

Ugly, thought Anna crossly and, her braids done, she thumped down off the chair, stalked out into the hall and ran into Papa.

Anna did not tell him what was wrong because already it was no longer true; nobody could feel ugly with Papa. He reached out, pulled a flower from a vase on the hall stand and stuck it behind his daughter's ear. It dripped water from its stem down her back but she laughed. Papa was so silly sometimes. Hastily, even while she grinned at him, she replaced the flower, hoping Mama would not notice.

"Well, how are you and Frau Schmidt getting along?" Papa asked.

Anna's smile vanished.

"All right," she muttered.

Anna knew he was not fooled by this. He had

spoken with Frau Schmidt on Visitors' Day. But soon it would be vacation time.

"Anna, my Anna, would you do a special favor for me?" her father asked suddenly.

Anna looked at him.

"Does it have anything to do with Frau Schmidt?"

He shook his head but his eyes twinkled. Anna did not quite believe him. Even the nicest adults could play tricks sometimes.

"Not one thing to do with Frau Schmidt, I swear!" Papa put his hand over his heart and looked solemnly up to heaven.

"What is it then?" probed Anna, stalling.

"Promise me first and then I'll tell," he wheedled. "Oh Anna, don't you trust your own Papa?"

Anna did not but she did love him more than anyone else in the entire world. She could not resist him.

"I promise then," she growled, in spite of herself. "Now tell me what it is?"

"I want you to try to speak English," Papa said.

Anna stiffened. She felt betrayed. But he was smiling at her again as though his words were not so dreadful.

"I do not think it will be quite so hard as you imagine," he told her gently. "Remember. You are the girl who learned all of 'Die Gedanken sind frei' in only one afternoon."

"But that was German!" protested Anna, knowing she had already promised but still hoping he had left her a loophole to wiggle through.

"But you were just five years old. Now you are much, much older and much, much smarter . . . and I suspect, though I might be wrong, that you already know much more English than you are letting on."

How had he guessed? Anna felt the telltale flush color her cheeks. She ducked her head so she would not have to meet his amused eyes. It was perfectly true. She had long since started storing away in her mind some of the strange words, although she had never yet dared speak them aloud. By now she could astonish him, if she chose. Would she?

"Ernst! Anna! You are going to be late for school," Mama called. "And there is a letter here for you from Canada, Ernst, which looks important."

They went. The letter lay at Papa's place. He opened it and read it. Then his hands clenched, half crumpling the page.

"What is it?" Mama cried, hurrying to him.

Papa had to wait a moment. Anna saw him swallow.

"My brother Karl is dead," he said then. "He had a heart attack. He has left me everything he owned."

There was a babble of voices.

"Oh, Papa, how awful!" said Gretchen, who remembered Uncle Karl from when she was a small girl and he had visited Germany and stayed with them.

"Papa, are we going to be rich then?" That was Rudi.

"Rich," Fritz echoed longingly but he stopped there. Something in Papa's face silenced him.

"Poor Papa," Frieda chimed in, kicking Fritz.

It was then that Papa said the unbelievable thing. He did not ask anyone. He just made a statement, a flat hard statement of fact.

"No, Rudi, we will not be rich. Karl was only a grocer with a small store, and Germany is not the only country which has been suffering from a depression. But this is our chance. We will go to Canada."

"Canada!"

In every voice there was the same feeling Anna had heard in Mama's months before. Canada was not a place to go to; Canada was a geography lesson.

"Mr. Menzies suggests we come in September." Papa went on as though he heard no outcry.

"Who is Mr. Menzies? What does he know about what we do?" Mama's words cut through the air as shrilly as a whistle.

"He's Karl's lawyer. I'd written to Karl before, asking what our chances would be in Canada. He offered to take us in but I wanted my own business. He said there was no place for a German English teacher. But now I shall be a grocer. I did not want Karl's charity but it seems he has given it to me after all."

Papa got up, letter in hand, and strode out of the room. There were tears on his cheeks. Anna saw them. She could not move. She could not think. Mama, though, started after him. Then, at the last minute, she saw the clock, gasped and stopped to hustle them off to school, refusing to answer any of the questions.

"Go! GO!" she almost screamed at them. "As though things aren't bad enough with this in your father's head!"

Suddenly, she caught sight of Anna, who still had not stirred from her chair. She looked at her hard—and it was not the warm look which claimed Anna as her "one German child." Anna shrank back, not understanding, not till her mother stormed, "Why is Germany not good enough for you? A land where thoughts are free! Bah! Oh, it is too much to bear. He cannot mean it."

She whirled away then and left them without her "Good-bye." As Anna went out, closing the door behind herself, she could hear Mama right through the walls.

"Ernst, Ernst, I will not go. I tell you *I will not go!*"

And then, pausing, she heard Papa, not so loudly, but in a voice like iron.

"We are all going, Klara. Whether you understand or not, whether you come willingly or not, we are going. You must start to get ready."

At school that day, Anna did not notice Frau Schmidt's gibes. She did not care what they sang in Assembly. She walked right past Herr Keppler in the hall, almost touching him, and she did not even notice.

They, her family, were going to Canada to live. And she had promised to try to speak English. Did everyone in Canada speak English?

Questions without answers hammered inside her

skull till she felt dizzy and sick. At last it was time to go home.

But home was not a good place to be either. There was no escape at home.

When Papa said they were going, he meant it. Rudi tried arguing, man to man. Papa listened.

"So you see, Papa, we can't go," Rudi finished.

"We *are* going, Rudi," his father said and went on making the arrangements.

Gretchen cried because she would have to leave her friend Maria.

"I've never had a friend like Maria, Papa," she sobbed. Gretchen, who was always so grown-up and calm.

Papa held her on his knee though she was much too big. She rested her head on his shoulder. Her tears wet his shirt collar and wilted it.

"You'll find another friend, my Gretel," Papa said.

Gretchen sprang away from him and went to howl on her bed.

Papa bought their tickets. They were going by steamship. It should have been exciting. To Fritz and Frieda it was. They began to brag.

But Papa even put a stop to that, the moment he found out about it.

"I don't want you talking about the fact that we are going," he told the whole family.

"If you'd only explain, Papa," Rudi answered, "then we'd know what to say. People ask us questions, you know. Herr Keppler himself was asking me this morning, but then he hadn't time to stay and listen. He will ask again."

"Oh, poor Rudi," Frieda breathed.

Rudi tossed his head.

"He doesn't scare me," he maintained.

"He should," Papa said in a low voice. But before they could ask what he meant this time, he gave his instructions in so decided a way that the discussion ended.

"You may tell people your uncle has died and we have been left a business in Canada. Say that I have to go and look after it. Say we have all decided to go. You don't need to say more than that. I do not want you to talk about it any more than you have to. If Herr Keppler does ask again, be careful and remember—what I am telling you is important. It is not safe to say too much."

Papa sounded so serious. The children knew there was much he was not telling them. Mama thought he was wrong, but even Rudi believed Papa. He was too unhappy himself to be doing it for some foolish reason. He even tried to get his sister Tania and her husband to come too. They agreed the Soldens should go, but did not want to go themselves.

"We have no children to think of, Ernst," Uncle Tobias said gravely. "Germany is our country, mine as much as yours. I would not desert it now."

"You may soon be left with no choice, Tobias," Papa said, deeply troubled.

"We know that," Aunt Tania said quietly. "But if all people of reason flee, who will speak the truth?"

Papa was silenced by that. That was when Anna knew he did not want to go either, that he was going because of his promise to her and because of his love for all of them—Rudi, Gretchen, the twins, even Mama who was still fighting against him.

Poor Papa!

English! She could talk English for him. That might cheer him. She had been meaning to try for days but she was afraid. They would laugh. Still, she could try. This very night, she would.

Supper was nearly ready. Rudi was sitting at the big round table, his fair head bent over the German–English dictionary. He was teaching them new words while they worked. The others stepped around him patiently. They were used to him finding an excuse to sit down when it was time to work. Mama was tight-lipped and silent as he read, but the rest knew by now that they were really going to need this new language so they were all listening.

"Awful" had been the last word. Anna repeated it silently, trying to keep hold of it.

Rudi read on down the page.

" 'Awkward.' What a queer word," he commented. "It means 'clumsy.' "

Somehow—Anna never knew how—the plate of sausages she was putting on the table chose that moment to slip through her fingers and shatter on the floor right by Rudi's feet.

He yelped as though she had fired off a cannon at

him. Then he saw it was only Anna and he felt foolish. Covering up quickly, he turned on her.

"Awkward," he said loudly. "That'll be easy to remember. We'll only need to think of you. Awkward Anna!"

Anna, on her knees picking up the mess, did not look up. If nobody answered him back, he might leave it at that. But Frieda, not being the one in danger, was not so careful.

"You broke a cup yourself just last week, Rudi," she cried. "How can you be so mean! Don't you dare call her that."

Rudi dared anything. He disliked being reminded of his own mistakes. And no eleven-year-old girl was going to order him around and get away with it.

"But think how it will help us with our English, dear Frieda," he said, his voice smooth as cream.

Anna felt cold.

He said no more then. Instead, he buried his nose in the dictionary again. By the time the meal was ready, he had found names for the other three as well.

Fearful Frieda came first. Frieda tossed her head in scorn at that. Then Fierce Fritz. Fritz grinned after he had checked to see what it meant. Glorious Gretchen was third. (Rudi had had to grab that one at the last minute because Mama said it was time to wash his hands and eat.) Gretchen just laughed.

Later, however, she did some looking on her own and at breakfast she came back at him with, "Would you like some more chocolate, Rude Rudi?"

Even Rudi grinned and the nicknames were dropped—except for Anna's. She knew herself why it stuck. Fritz put it into words when she fell headlong over a footstool a couple of days later.

"There goes Awkward Anna," he commented. Then he looked ashamed. "It's just that it fits her so," he excused himself to Papa.

Soon it was accepted by them all. They said it with a shake of their heads. They even said it fondly. But they said it. Rudi said it most often; he guessed how much it hurt. Only Papa never used it; he guessed too.

Anna could not win with Rudi. She had learned that when she was still little more than a baby.

Now she no longer wanted to amaze Papa with her knowledge of English. English was tied to that awful word which followed her everywhere:

Awkward. Awkward.

How she hated it! How she believed it was true!

In spite of herself, she went on learning new words as the weeks passed. Mama, suddenly and to everyone's astonishment, gave in and began to speak the new language along with the rest. No longer was Anna special in her silence. Now it angered her mother.

"It is time to stop this stubbornness, Anna," she said. "I am old but I am learning. We must do what we must do." Tears came to her eyes as she spoke.

Anna turned away. Mama would never understand.

And Anna need not feel guilty about making her mother cry. Mama cried every day now. She cried as she packed.

"You cannot take everything with you, Klara," Papa told her, and he made her give Aunt Tania the soup tureen.

Anna thought that was silly. Crying over a soup tureen. It was uglier than she was, even, with its silly little cupids holding up the handle and its curly feet and its big awkwardness.

That word again!

"I've had it since I was a bride," Mama wept, and Aunt Tania wept with her.

After that, Papa had to give in about the mantel clock which chimed every quarter hour. It had belonged to Mama's mother. Papa knew when he was beaten. Anna was glad this time. She loved the clock's musical chime. Lying in bed listening to it was one of the first things she remembered.

The last day of school came.

"Well, Anna, so you are leaving us," Frau Schmidt said. She did not sound sorry. "I hope you will work hard for your new teacher."

Her voice said she doubted it. Anna said only, "Yes, Frau Schmidt."

But as she was going down the hall carrying her things, another voice stopped her.

"Anna," said Fräulein Braun, catching up to her, "I hope you weren't going without saying good-bye."

Anna looked at her blankly. Fräulein Braun taught music, and Anna liked music. But she had not imagined the music teacher had noticed her.

"I'll miss you," Fräulein Braun said gently. "You have a very nice voice, Anna, and you sing as though you meant the words."

"I . . . Thank you," Anna stammered. "Good-bye, Fräulein."

For one instant, she was sorry to be leaving school behind.

Then finally it was time. They were going tomorrow, away from their home, to a land where people spoke English.

Anna had made a vow never, ever to speak it, no matter what she had promised Papa. But how was she going to be able to keep that vow in Canada?

Everything was packed. They sat on boxes to eat their last meal in Frankfurt.

"It feels lonely here," Frieda whispered, her eyes huge.

Papa laughed all at once. It was as though he had been afraid to laugh for a long time, but now, suddenly, his fear was vanishing. He could see where he was taking them and it was a fine, safe place.

"Let's not be lonely," he rallied them. "Why, we all have each other. We can make a fresh start together, we Soldens. We just need some courage. What's the bravest song you know?"

It was Gretchen who said it, not Anna.

" 'Die Gedanken sind frei,' Papa," she cried.

Anna felt much braver as their voices chased back the shadows and filled the emptiness with joyous sound.

> Die Gedanken sind frei,
> *My thoughts freely flower.*
> Die Gedanken sind frei,
> *My thoughts give me power.*
> *No scholar can map them.*
> *No hunter can trap them . . .*

Suddenly, her voice faltered and broke off. Nobody else had seen, but Mama was crying again. Her cheeks were wet with tears. As the others swept on into the wonderful second verse and the triumphant finish, Anna once more felt alone and afraid. Then she saw her father smile at her mother and she looked at Mama again.

The tears were still there but Mama was singing as bravely as anyone.

4 • "PAPA IS WRONG!"

The first day out at sea, everyone but Anna was sick. Papa, looking pale and refusing to eat, did manage to stay on his feet and go with his youngest child to dinner in the grand dining salon. But the rest, even Rudi, lay groaning in their bunks.

Anna could not understand it. She herself felt fine. Better than fine. Wonderful! She loved keeping her balance while the floor rocked beneath her feet. On land she was always tripping and stumbling, but here, when the ship rolled, she let her body sway with it, shifting her weight to match its rhythm. She never had to catch hold of something to steady herself. On her own two feet she was steadier than anyone, even Papa. If only the others were not too sick to notice!

She loved the giant thrum of the ship's engine too and the different feeling everywhere. Maybe she was a new, a different Anna. In the dining room, ordering her dinner from a huge menu she could not read, she sat up like a queen and she felt new and powerful in spite of the stupid menu.

"Have something with me, Papa," she coaxed.

Papa smiled at her open happiness but he shook his head at the mere mention of food. Anna ate quickly, guessing rightly that if he had to face her beef dinner for long, he also might desert her. It was too bad. Here they were alone together, and yet it was spoiled. Now her father had actually shut his eyes!

Suddenly, she had an inspiration. She had still not started to use English, although as they drew nearer and nearer to Canada, she knew she could not put it off much longer. Why not try now? It was the perfect moment, with only Papa here to listen and be delighted and not laugh if she made a mistake.

She thought furiously. She could ask, "When will we get to Canada?"

No. He would know she already knew the answer. Something else, something clever. . . .

"Are you finished, Anna?" her father said, seeing she had stopped eating and was staring into space. He pushed his chair back a little. "I'd like to see how your mother is."

Anna knew exactly how Mama was. She was doubled up in a ball and she did not want to be spoken to. When Mama had a headache at home, Gretchen usually fussed over her, bringing her drinks of water, turning her pillow, pulling down the shade. But now Gretchen herself was ill. Anna, suddenly important but shy about it, had asked in a small, self-conscious voice, "Mama, would you like some water?"

Mama had not even turned her head. "No, no. Leave me in peace," she had moaned. Then she had added, "And speak English, Anna."

Now Papa was waiting for her to come. "Anna, did you hear me?" he asked when she did not move.

The excitement which had been blossoming inside his daughter closed up as tightly as a flower when darkness nears. Anna pushed back her own chair and stood up.

"I am finished," she said in curt German.

"Being sick is so hard for them," her father commented as he led the way through a maze of tables.

The words were in English. Papa hardly ever spoke German now.

He must know that I understand, Anna thought as she followed him down the passageway.

Yet only that once, weeks before, had he asked her to try to speak English. And she had promised she would. She could not remember ever before having promised Papa anything and then breaking her word.

Why didn't he say something, remind her, even scold her?

He knows that I remember, thought Anna. But he guesses that I am afraid.

Saying the very first words aloud, that was what she could not seem to manage. She had tried, but every time they stuck in her throat. She was sure that when she did speak, her English would come out twisted and sounding ridiculous. Mama made terrible mistakes all the time. The family tried not to laugh at her, but sometimes they could not help it. Rudi would be merciless when Anna's turn came.

So she made up English sentences inside her head and even whispered them under her breath sometimes when she was alone, but when anybody was listening, she continued to talk only German.

The next morning the sun shone, the sea was calm, and the Soldens recovered. After breakfast the five children set out to explore the ship. Papa frowned as he watched them go. He did not like the way Anna trailed along behind, not quite one with the rest. Were the older ones unkind to her?

He settled down in his deck chair and opened a book. Klara, stretched out next to him, was already half asleep in the sunshine.

She is coming around at last, he thought with relief. That will make things easier for Anna.

"What's the trouble, Ernst?" she asked lazily.

"Nothing," he told her. Then, in spite of himself,

he added, "It was just Anna. The rest didn't seem to want her."

Klara Solden's eyes flashed open.

"And why should they want her?" she challenged. "She's so touchy these days. She's not making any effort to adjust. . . . She can't hear me, can she?" Her face was suddenly anxious as she pushed herself up on one elbow and looked around.

"No, no. They've gone," her husband reassured her.

He smiled as she lay back and let her eyes close again. But a moment later, he put down his book and got to his feet.

"What now?" his wife asked as he moved away.

"I'm just going to check on what they're up to," Papa called back, walking a bit faster. "You never know with that Fritz."

Anna, following the rest, was not unhappy though. Not yet. It was too glorious a day. The blueness and bigness of the sky made her want to sing. And everything was still new. There was still a chance that she might not be Awkward Anna any longer.

Then the twins discovered some metal hand rails. In an instant, the four older children were competing with each other like circus acrobats. They hung by their hands and then their knees. They skinned the cat, flipping themselves over with ease. They held their feet off the ground and went the length of the rails hand over hand. Fritz shinnied up a post, winding himself around it like a pretzel.

"Try this, Rudi!" he yelled down from high above them.

Anna stood and watched. She was too full of admiration for her brothers and sisters to feel sorry for herself. These daring, agile creatures swinging and laughing and climbing in the sunlight belonged to her, even though she was not like them.

Papa spoke from right behind her, startling her so that she almost lost her balance.

"Why aren't you playing with them, Anna?" he asked.

Anna looked up at him helplessly. She couldn't explain. What would she say? That she was too stupid? That she would fall? That she didn't know how?

He was waiting for an answer. The brightness of the morning dimmed.

Gretchen, flushed from hanging upside down, came running over to see what Papa wanted and saved her.

"Why don't you let Anna play too?" Papa asked before Gretchen could say a word.

It was not a fair question. Gretchen looked at her stocky younger sister. Anna should speak up and tell Papa that she *wouldn't* play. Not that they had asked her this time, but they hadn't asked each other either.

Anna said nothing. She had her head turned away a little.

"Nobody's stopping her, Papa," Gretchen said. "Really and truly, I don't think she wants to play. She's hopeless at things like this. She's too big . . . or maybe too little."

Gretchen's words halted. Anna was not quite as tall as Frieda but still she was, somehow, too big. They had all seen her fall many times. She landed heavily and often got up so clumsily that she tripped again.

As Gretchen gave up in despair, Fritz joined them for a fleeting instant. He caught enough of the conversation to offer a quick opinion.

"If Anna practiced, like me and Frieda, she'd be better. But she won't, so it's her own fault she's Awkward Anna."

He dashed off again before Papa could speak. Gretchen wanted to go too, Anna knew, but she waited.

"You should remember Anna is the youngest and help her, Gretel," said Papa.

Gretchen went redder than ever.

"We *have* tried!" she burst out. "Papa, she doesn't want to do our things. Really she doesn't."

At last Anna's silence reached her father. What was he doing to her? Ignoring Gretchen, he turned and asked gently, "Anna, would you like to come for a walk with your Papa?"

Anna did not want pity, not even his.

"I have something else I must do right now," she lied, not looking at either her father or her sister. Keeping her head high, her back straight, she walked away. A lifeboat stood nearby. She strode quickly around it. Once out of sight, she stood still with nowhere to go, nothing to do but ache inside.

Then she discovered she was still within earshot.

"Oh, Papa," she heard Gretchen wail, "why is it

that Anna makes you feel so mean when you know you haven't been?"

Anna tensed, ready for more hurt.

"I know it isn't always easy," Papa said slowly, thinking his way. "But, Gretchen, there is something special in our Anna. One day you will see that I am right. She has so much love locked up in her."

"Yes, Papa," Gretchen said, her voice flat.

But Anna had forgotten her big sister. On the far side of the lifeboat, she was standing in a new world, carried there by her father's words.

Had she really heard Papa?

Special!

She was not certain of the rest but she was sure Papa had used that word about her, Anna.

Not "different." She hated being different. Special, though, was something else. It meant wonderful, didn't it? It meant better than other people.

Slowly, Anna wandered on down the deck, pondering over this magical word. It shone. It sang inside her. It made the day beautiful again.

But was it true?

She stood still again, thinking hard.

She did not look special, she knew. She was too big and not one bit pretty.

And there were all those things she could not do: sew or knit or dust to suit Mama, play games, read even easy books.

She could sing in tune. She even had a nice voice.

Fräulein Braun had said so. But all the others sang as well as she did.

Yet Papa had said "something special."

Suddenly, just ahead of her, she saw another railing like the one the older children had been playing on. She could not have tried earlier with them watching her but now with Papa's words still sounding in her heart, with this feeling of newness which being on shipboard had given her, and with nobody to see and laugh, maybe she could do it. Then she could go back and show them. She would not say anything. She would just swing herself over as though she had always done it.

Maybe.

Anna Solden marched forward to the metal railing. She grasped it tightly, her palms already slippery from tension. Scrabbling with her feet, she tried to turn herself over between her hands the way her brothers and sisters did. She got one foot off the ground—and felt herself slipping.

"I can do it. I can. I *can!*" she grunted desperately.

But something in the way she was holding on was wrong. There must be some trick to it. Her grip gave way and she landed on the hard deck in a tangle of banged elbows and knees.

She lay, for an instant, wondering whether to try again. But she did not know what mistake she had made the first time.

She stood up quickly and yanked her dress straight.

Then she just ran, ran away, ran anywhere. She knocked into a pillar and bruised her shin on a stack of deck chairs but she did not stop. At last she reached a stretch of deck where there was nobody, not even a stranger in the distance. Panting, she leaned against a wall.

The sun still shone. The sky was still as big and as blue. Yet the joy in Anna had died.

"He is wrong," she cried out to a sea gull winging by. "Papa is wrong about me."

There was desolation in her voice but the gull paid no heed and no one else was near enough to hear—even though Anna, without noticing, had just spoken her first English words out loud.

5 • ANNA FINDS A FRIEND

"Mr. Menzies said he'd be here," Papa said.

The Soldens, just off the train, looked around wearily. Everywhere there were strangers. No one man stepped forward to say he was Mr. Menzies, Uncle Karl's lawyer.

"Menzies," muttered Mama. "It is not a German name."

"Klara, we are in Canada now," Papa said. The tartness in his voice startled the tired children. Papa was not the one who snapped.

"He must be here somewhere," he went on after a moment of strained silence.

The family stood in a huddle near the barriers in the waiting room at Toronto Union Station. After leaving the ship in Halifax, they had come the rest of the way by train. There had not been money enough for berths. Anna had sat up for thirty-six hours, leaning against Papa whenever she dozed, and now she swayed on her feet. If only she could lie down somewhere!

"He'll be here any minute," Papa spoke again, anxiously scanning the faces of people near them.

Anna had let her heavy eyelids close for just one second. Now she opened them wide in astonishment. Papa had spoken in German!

He must really be worried.

Anna did not stop to wonder whether she was right. She just went to his rescue in the only way she knew, butting up against him like a rude little goat, letting him know she was right there.

"Take care, Anna," Mama scolded. "If you're too tired to stand up, sit on the big suitcase."

Papa, though, smiled down into his daughter's anxious face.

"He's tall with red hair," he told her quietly.

Anna turned to look but before she saw more than a forest of legs clumped about with luggage, Mr. Menzies was there.

"Ernst Solden?"

"Yes, yes. You must be Mr. Menzies."

The men shook hands. Mr. Menzies was tall but his hair was more gray than red.

"My wife, Klara," Papa began introducing them.

"My oldest boy, Rudolf . . . Gretchen . . . Fritz and Elfrieda, our twins . . . and this is Anna."

Anna blinked at hearing Rudi and Frieda called by their real names. Mr. Menzies smiled politely.

"You two certainly look like your father," he told the older ones. "And the twins are very like you, Mrs. Solden."

Anna was startled again. She had never heard her mother called Mrs. before. Of course, it meant the same as Frau, but it made Mama seem a stranger.

"Anna," Papa said quickly, "is lucky enough to look like nobody but herself."

The lawyer looked at the youngest Solden and cleared his throat.

He doesn't know what to say next, Anna thought with scorn.

"Of course," the tall man murmured and turned back to Papa. "Did you have something to eat on the train?"

The adult talk went on over Anna's head. It was of no interest. This Canadian was like most of the other grown-ups she had met. He did not like her. Well, she did not like him either.

Moving automatically, she followed the others out of the station, across the street and into a restaurant. There she munched on a sandwich—something she had never eaten before—and sipped from a tall glass of milk.

"Are you sure you wouldn't rather stay in a hotel until tomorrow, anyway?" Mr. Menzies was asking.

"Are there still people in the house?" Papa said.

People in their new house? Anna came almost awake to hear the answer.

"No. Mr. Solden's tenants left last week—and I *was* able to buy some furniture from them, as you hoped. They were glad to get the cash. It isn't very good stuff . . ."

The lawyer sounded worried. Ernst Solden laughed.

"Right now, all we want are enough beds to go around. Good, bad, or indifferent, we don't care, do we, Klara?"

Mama murmured agreement but she did not sound as sure and carefree about it as Papa did.

"Did the two big trunks come with the bedding and dishes?" she asked.

"Yes, I had them delivered to the house. If only my wife hadn't been ill," Mr. Menzies worried on, "she would have gone over to see the place was clean. These people Karl had there were foreigners, you know. They . . ."

He stopped suddenly and reddened. Papa laughed again.

"Foreigners, is it?" he repeated. "It is all right, Mr. Menzies. We speak that way in Germany also. If the house is empty and the bedding has arrived, we should be fine. We can clean the house."

"The food tastes queer, doesn't it?" Frieda whispered to Anna then, and Anna stopped trying to follow what the adults were saying.

She nodded and made a face over her next bite, although really she did not notice anything wrong with it.

"You're crazy," Fritz told his twin. "Here. Give it to me."

Food was one of the few things over which the twins differed. Fritz gobbled up whatever was put before him. Frieda fussed and nibbled. Yet they both were thin and wiry. Anna, who ate more than Frieda but less than Fritz, was stocky and had big bones.

"Like a little ox," Mama sometimes teased.

"Franz Schumacher said he'd meet us here," Mr. Menzies was explaining to her parents. "He was a great friend of Karl's."

Mama beamed. Schumacher was a good German name. Franz, too.

"We'll need two cars to get you and your bags to the house. He's late. A last-minute patient, I suppose."

The words blurred in Anna's head. She dropped her sandwich half-eaten. By the time Dr. Schumacher came hurrying in, she was sound asleep in her chair. This time, she missed the introductions. She did not rouse until a deep voice, close beside her, said, "I'll carry this little one."

Mama objected. "She is much too heavy to carry. Wake her up. Anna . . . Anna!"

I can't, Anna thought groggily, keeping her eyes shut.

Strong arms gathered her up.

"She's not heavy at all," Dr. Schumacher grunted, shifting her to get a better grip. Anna flicked open her eyes for one split second, just long enough to see the big, friendly face. What had he said? Could she really have heard?

If the doctor knew she was awake, he made no sign. "Light as a feather—really!" he said to Mama.

Anna lay perfectly still in his arms. She kept her eyes tightly closed and she did not smile.

Yet she loved Franz Schumacher from that moment.

6 • HALF A HOUSE

Franz Schumacher was panting before he reached his car, but he did not put Anna down.

As they followed him, Frieda poked Fritz. "She's not really asleep," she whispered.

"Anybody can tell that," Fritz agreed. Then he shrugged. "With Anna, who knows why?" he murmured.

Frieda nodded and hurried to keep up to the others.

"I'll take Mr. Solden and the boys and the two big bags," Mr. Menzies suggested as Dr. Schumacher, still clutching Anna, halted and looked helplessly at his car.

"The door's locked," he explained.

Mama did not waste words. She grabbed Anna's dangling arm and gave it a good shake.

"Enough of this, Anna," she said in abrupt German. "You are not sleeping. Get down and stand on your own feet."

Anna opened her eyes as slowly as she dared. She yawned widely, innocently, like a kitten. Staying limp till the last possible moment, she allowed herself to be set on the pavement. Dr. Schumacher smiled at her as he released her but Anna was aware of the scorn her family felt.

"Anybody would be tired out after a long trip like that," the doctor said, backing her up. He sounded serious but his eyes twinkled.

He knows I wasn't really sleeping, Anna thought, and he doesn't mind.

Dr. Schumacher turned and began to open car doors.

"In here, Anna," he directed. "I'm afraid you'll have to squeeze over to make room."

Anna squeezed, but still there was not room enough. Mama pulled her.

"Come. You will have to sit on my knees," she said.

Anna obeyed but this time she did know she was too heavy. She tried to make herself lighter, to perch on the very edge of her mother's lap. The car started with a jerk. Anna crashed backward, and Mama gasped as the breath was knocked out of her. The girl braced herself but her mother, when she had breath enough to speak, had controlled her temper. She closed her lips tightly and shifted to adjust herself to Anna's weight.

They drove and drove. Lights were coming on in the houses they passed but they were dimmed by drawn curtains. The streets were empty and gray with dusk. Anna peered out into the shadows but she saw nothing comforting, no single bright thing which said, "Welcome to Canada!" Her throat ached with sudden misery.

"It looks lonely," Mama murmured.

Gretchen, sitting in the middle with luggage on her far side, did not answer. Maybe she, too, was remembering the small streets in Frankfurt where the Soldens knew and were known by everyone. Even fat Frau Meyer, who complained so about the noise they made when they played outside, seemed a friend now that they would never see her again.

For an instant, Anna's mind wandered, picturing their neighbors—Trudi, the downstairs baby, who was not quite walking when they left; Maria Schliemann, Gretchen's best friend; Herr Gunderson . . .

Suddenly, her mind jerked forward again to the present. Had Mama actually said it looked lonely? Frieda was chattering to Dr. Schumacher. The old car rattled and roared. Maybe she had merely imagined she heard Mama speak.

She twisted halfway around and tried to read her mother's expression. If Mama was lonely, Anna did not know what to do.

Her mother's face stayed masked in shadow.

Gretchen, say something to Mama, Anna wished.

Then the car stopped at an intersection, directly under a streetlight. Klara Solden lifted her head and smiled brightly at Anna and at Gretchen too.

"We will be there soon, children, very soon," she told them in her choppy English. "We are almost at our new home."

As if we didn't know that! Anna scoffed to herself, turning her back on her mother again.

Mama's loud, too-cheerful voice made the twilight lonelier than ever.

"You must be so excited, both," Mama forged ahead. "This is a wonderful chance for you, Gretchen . . . and Anna too . . . seeing another country . . . while you are still only young."

Mama did not sound as though she believed a word she herself was saying. Anna stared out at the darkening street. It was not up to her to answer, even if she knew what to say. Gretchen would do it. Gretchen, Mama's pet, would know exactly the right words to comfort their mother. Anna waited.

Gretchen said nothing.

Forget Maria, Anna stormed at her without making a sound. Say something. Say something to Mama.

Gretchen coughed, a small hard cough.

Then, seconds late, she at last responded to Mama's rallying speech.

"Yes, Mama, of course we are excited," she said. "It will all be very nice, I'm sure."

Now Gretchen's voice was unnaturally loud, desperately bright, just like Mama's. Anna stiffened with anger at the pair of them. Why couldn't they be their usual calm, irritating selves? Why did they have to be so brave?

Frieda, in the middle of telling Dr. Schumacher how she and Fritz had won a singing prize when they were seven, looked over her shoulder at her older sister.

"What did you say, Gretchen?" she asked.

"I was speaking to Mama." Gretchen's voice was flat now.

"Did Mama say something?" Frieda questioned, not wanting to be left out.

"It is all right, Frieda. Never mind," her mother told her. Then she reached out and squeezed Gretchen's hands, which were clenched together in her lap.

"Thank you, daughter," she said softly. "I know you are trying. Right now . . . right now, you are the dearest child."

That was the last straw. It had been a long time since Mama had called any of them "the dearest child," and Anna, without letting herself think about it, had been thankful. It was a family tradition, something Mama had done since before Anna could remember. Mama always assured them she loved each of them equally. All five were precious. None was her favorite. Yet once in a while, one child did do something extra special and was Mama's "dearest child" for that one moment.

Everyone liked this—everyone but Anna.

She knew, and so did the others, that she had never really been "the dearest child." Oh, Mama called her that now and then, but always when Anna did something Mama asked her to do, like setting the table or going to the store. Anna tried not to care, of course. She often told herself how little she cared. Still, it had been nice when Mama stopped bothering. Since Papa announced they would go to Canada, Mama did not seem to notice special moments.

And what's so wonderful about stupid old Gretchen this time? Anna silently asked the world. She's being good on purpose.

Mama and Gretchen were talking softly now in German but Anna would not give in and listen. She did not want to hear Gretchen being . . .

Grown-up, thought Anna.

But that was silly. Gretchen was only thirteen. Not grown-up at all.

"Here we are," Dr. Schumacher said and parked the car.

They unfolded themselves and climbed out.

"There," the doctor pointed.

"The whole house?" Mama gasped.

It had been years since they had had a house to themselves. Not since Gretchen was a baby and they lived in a cottage.

But Frieda looked more closely.

"It's half a house," she said. "There are people in the other half."

"Yes. You share one wall with your neighbors," the doctor agreed. "But it really is a separate house."

Mama suddenly sighed. It sounded almost like a sob. This time, Gretchen did have the right words ready.

"It will be better with lights in the windows, Mama," she said.

"I know," Klara Solden answered, struggling to sound convinced.

Then the other car pulled up and Papa was there. As Mama turned to him, somehow she made her smile real.

"Our new home, Ernst," she said.

Papa now stood and stared at the tall, narrow slice of house which was theirs.

"What did Karl want with a place this size?" he wondered aloud.

"Oh, he didn't live here. He rented it. He boarded with a family next door to the store. I don't know why he bought this place but I'm afraid it is pretty run-down," Mr. Menzies explained.

Papa nodded his head thoughtfully.

"Yes, of course, I remember. Karl planned to marry years ago. Gerda Hertz . . . but she would not wait. Let us go in."

It was a dirty house. It was dark and smelled closed-in and musty. Their feet crunched grittily as they crowded into the downstairs hall. Anna pushed close to Papa again, this time wanting reassurance herself. He set down the large suitcase he was carrying

and put one hand on top of her head. It rested there for only a moment. That was enough. Anna moved quickly away before the others had time to notice.

Mr. Menzies went from room to room, switching on lights. The Soldens followed in his wake. This was not a house to explore by yourself.

They had been upstairs for several minutes before anyone realized that they were one bedroom short. There was a room downstairs with a huge double bed. That was clearly Mama's and Papa's room. There was a small room in the front of the house upstairs. It was small because the bathroom next to it ate into its space. It too held a double bed—and there was no room for anything much else. A dresser had been crowded in behind the bed but you could only open the drawers halfway. Nobody demanded that room.

Rudi claimed the only other bedroom though, the instant they entered it.

"This must be where Fritz and I belong," he said.

He dumped his armload of bundles down on the better looking of the two sagging single beds.

"But, Rudi," Gretchen began.

She stopped in mid-sentence. Rudi was eldest.

"All right. Come on, Frieda," she sighed, glancing back at the first room with distaste.

"But Papa," Frieda said then. "Look. There's no place for Anna."

7 • ANNA'S PLACE

Frieda looked sorry a moment later.

"It isn't that I wouldn't share with you, Anna," she hurried to say, her brown eyes hoping her sister would understand. "But there's just one bed—and I had you all the way over on the ship."

She grinned, trying to make Anna smile too.

"I could show you the bruises," she said.

Anna could not answer. What was there to say? She knew she was a restless sleeper. On the ship Frieda had often poked her awake and ordered her to stop thrashing around in the narrow berth they had shared.

Here there *must* be someplace though. There had to be.

"I've found something," Dr. Schumacher called. His voice echoed eerily in to them from the dark hall. Relieved, they went to see. Anna walked slowly, her back very straight, her head higher than high.

It was not a room really. It was a bite out of the hall with one side open, a space left between the other two bedrooms.

"An alcove," Mr. Menzies said.

Anna swallowed. It was dark in there and there was no window. A narrow cot stood against the wall, though. Someone had used it as a bedroom before.

"Anna is too little to sleep out here all alone," Mama said, her voice troubled.

"She can't sleep with Frieda and *me*, if that's what you're thinking," Gretchen burst out. She was tired of being the brave, kind, big sister. She spoke sharply, without kindness. "You know how she is, Mama. She even moans sometimes!"

Anger flared up in Anna, saving her. Something like pity in Dr. Schumacher's face helped fan the flame.

"I *want* to sleep here. I *want* to be by myself," she declared fiercely. "I hate having to share—especially with them!"

Klara Solden's temper caught fire as quickly as Anna's.

"Fine," she snapped, all softness gone. "This shall be Anna's room. And nobody will disturb her. Remember that. We shall wait to be asked."

The others murmured uneasy assent. The older children were busy looking at their feet suddenly. There was something about Anna's aloneness that they did not want to see. Papa cleared his throat.

"Papa," Anna warned under her breath before he could begin.

He stopped, peered down at her, and cleared his throat again.

"What is it, Ernst?" Mama asked crossly.

"Nothing," Papa said. "We'll get you a special chest to hold your things, Anna."

"All right," Anna said in a dull, colorless voice, as though it did not matter much one way or the other.

Papa suddenly took charge.

"Baths for everyone, Klara," he ordered. "I'll find that box of bedding for you. These children are sleeping on their feet."

"I'll need something to clean that bathtub," Mama responded, beginning gallantly to attempt the impossible. "Gretta, you come and help me. Oh, this place needs cleaning so."

"Tomorrow we'll get properly settled," Papa called after her. "It will look better in daylight. . . . What about food for breakfast?" he remembered, turning back to Mr. Menzies.

Mr. Menzies looked helpless. "My wife . . ." he began and stopped.

Dr. Schumacher came up with the answer.

"You'll find plenty at the store," he said. "Do you have the key, John? We could go now."

Mr. Menzies produced the key, and the three men started for the stairs.

"When you do get settled and a bit rested," the doctor said, "bring the children around to my office to have their medical examinations for school."

"School!" Fritz echoed, horrified.

The doctor looked back at the boy and laughed.

"Yes, school," he said. "It starts a week from Tuesday."

Fritz groaned.

The men went on downstairs, Dr. Schumacher explaining on the way where his office was.

"Come on, Fritz," Rudi ordered. The boys disappeared into their new room. Frieda ran after them.

Anna stood in the hall alone. She could hear the men's voices rumbling below, Rudi telling the twins how "his" room would be arranged, water running into the bathtub.

Gretchen came back through the hall. Mama had sent her in search of towels.

The older girl almost tripped over Anna, who still stood by herself in the alcove which was to be her bedroom. Gretchen paused. She looked at her little sister. Standing there, alone, she seemed to be crying aloud for help. But Gretchen knew Anna. It was not that easy. She was as difficult to get close to as a porcupine. It was no use asking her what was wrong. She would never tell.

Besides, Gretchen thought, there's so much wrong. I hate it here too. We should never have come to this awful place.

"Gretchen, are you coming?" Mama called.

"Yes, Mama. In a minute!" Gretchen called back.

She took two steps toward the stairs. Behind her, Anna stood not moving, not speaking. In spite of herself, knowing it was useless, Gretchen turned back.

"Anna, it's not so bad . . ." she started.

"Mama wants you," Anna interrupted. "You'd better go. You're standing in my room, anyway, and I didn't ask you in."

"You . . . are . . . *impossible!*" Gretchen spat the words at the younger girl.

She whirled away and ran down the stairs.

"Papa!" Anna heard her calling. "Mama wants towels."

She was alone again. She backed up and sat down carefully on the extreme edge of the rickety cot. She sat very still, with her arms hugged in close around herself.

School—a week from Tuesday!

She should have known, of course. She should have seen it coming. Yet somehow, in all the rush of the packing and the weeks of travel, she had never thought that far ahead. Not once had she pictured herself actually going to school in a strange land.

School had been terrible enough back in Frankfurt. Anna sat in the darkness and remembered Frau Schmidt. Now it was going to start again, only this time it would be one hundred times worse. It would be in English.

When Mama came bustling in search of her, Anna had not moved.

"Anna Elisabeth Solden, get up from there and undress for your bath. What's the matter with you?" Mama jerked at her, getting her onto her feet. "I'll have the bed made by the time you're finished. Here, let me help."

Anna freed herself. "I can do it," she said.

Mama's hands dropped to her sides. She sighed. Then she frowned. Anna was moving—but so slowly.

"Speak English," her mother commanded suddenly.

Maybe she too was thinking of school beginning. Maybe she too was afraid for Anna, her one German child.

"I will not," Anna said in German. The words grated in her throat.

Then she turned her back on her mother and pulled her dress up over her head. Whatever Mama said next, she could not hear.

8 • DR. SCHUMACHER'S DISCOVERY

Dr. Schumacher's waiting room was shabby and crowded. When the Soldens arrived, the two boys had to stand up against one wall with their father because there were not enough chairs.

"All right," Dr. Schumacher smiled, "who's first?"

Rudi stepped forward. Mama got up to go with him. He scowled at her.

"I'm not a baby," he muttered, sounding like Anna.

"Let him go in by himself, Klara," Papa said. "Go ahead, Rudi." He came over and, taking Anna on his knee to make room, sat on the bench beside his wife.

"It will be fine," he told her. "Wait. You'll see."

Mama was not convinced. She was used to taking her children to the doctor only when they were sick. Gretchen had to have her tonsils out when she was three. Fritz had those bad earaches. And Rudi had broken his arm falling out of a tree he had been told not to climb. But for most things Mama did not need a doctor to tell her what to do. She had her own remedies for sore throats and skinned knees, stomachaches, and even measles. They all had injections before they came to Canada, but that had been so hurried that she had no time to think about it. Suppose this doctor she did not know found one of her children had some dread disease?

"I don't trust these foreign doctors," she muttered now at Papa.

"Klara, we're the foreigners here!" he reminded her, speaking quietly but not bothering to whisper. "Besides, Franz Schumacher is as German as you are."

Mama shook her head—but there stood Rudi, grinning.

"One healthy one!" Dr. Schumacher said. "You're next—Gretchen, is it?"

This time Mama sat still, although her eyes followed Gretchen every step of the way until the door closed behind her.

"Do you think she looked pale?" she asked Papa.

Ernst Solden laughed, a big laugh that filled the room. "Gretchen—pale! She has cheeks like roses and you know it."

Anna snuggled closer to him and laughed too. It was funny thinking of Gretchen as pale.

"She was green on the ship," she offered.

"Now, Anna, that is not tactful," her father said. "Just because you were the only sensible one . . ."

Mama shushed them both sternly.

Papa chuckled again and gave Anna an extra squeeze.

Gretchen came back, her cheeks as rosy as ever. Frieda went and returned. Fritz was a couple of minutes longer.

"Maybe something is wrong with Fritz . . ." Mama began, her eyes growing wide.

"He let me listen to my own heart," Fritz bragged, bouncing out into the waiting room.

"A fine family, you Soldens," Dr. Schumacher boomed, stretching out a broad hand to Anna. She slid off her father's knee at once, and put her hand in the doctor's. Papa smiled. So someone else had discovered a way to reach his Anna!

As they disappeared, Mama gave a deep sigh of relief.

"Didn't I tell you?" her husband teased.

She had to nod. Only Anna was left—and Anna had not been seriously ill in her entire life.

"Let me hear you read the letters on this card," Dr. Schumacher was saying to the youngest of the Soldens.

Anna froze. Reading! She couldn't . . .

She looked where he was pointing. Why, there was

only one letter there. That was easy! She did know the names of the letters now.

"E" she told him.

"And the next line down?" Dr. Schumacher asked.

Anna wrinkled up her forehead. Yes, there *were* other letters. She could see them now, when she squinted. They looked like little gray bugs, wiggling.

"They're too small to read," she said.

Ten minutes later, when he had made very sure, the doctor came out to the waiting room with the little girl.

"Did you know that this child can't see?" he asked sternly.

Ernst and Klara Solden's blank faces told him the answer. Feeling sorry then, he tried to soften his voice, although he was still angry on Anna's behalf.

"At least she can't see much," he corrected himself.

Mama snatched at Anna. Had Anna known it, at that moment she was the only one who mattered. For once she was actually "the dearest child." But Anna did not guess. She pulled away from her mother's anxious hands and stood out of reach.

"Of course she can see!" Klara Solden gasped, turning away from the child to this foreign doctor whom she had not trusted from the beginning. "What do you mean? Don't be ridiculous!"

The doctor looked from one of Anna's parents to the other.

"She sees very poorly, very poorly indeed," he said. "She should be wearing glasses. She probably should have had them two or three years ago. But before we go any further, I want to have her examined by an oculist . . . an eye doctor."

This time Mama would not be left behind. The others stayed in Dr. Schumacher's waiting room while Anna was taken upstairs to see Dr. Milton. Mama sniffed with scorn at this name, but she was too frightened to make any added protest.

It was all like a nightmare to Anna. Once more, she had to read letters off a faraway card. Once again, she could only see the big E. The new doctor peered into her eyes with a small bright light. He made her look through a collection of lenses. All at once, other letters appeared.

"F . . . P," Anna read in a low voice. "T . . . O, I think . . . Z."

"Now these," Dr. Milton said, pointing to the next row of letters. But they were too small.

Dr. Milton clucked his tongue. He began to talk to Mama in rapid English. Mama threw up her hands and rattled German back at him. Dr. Milton took them back down to Dr. Schumacher's office and the two doctors talked. The Soldens waited anxiously, Anna looking sullen, her usual touchy, difficult self. She was trying, inside, to pretend that she was not there. It was not helping.

Dr. Schumacher took her to yet another room where she sat on a chair and was fitted for frames.

"What a nice little girl," the optometrist said heartily.

Anna glowered.

"Even with the glasses, she will not have normal vision," Franz Schumacher explained when they were back in his office. The grown-ups took the chairs. Anna stood near Papa but she did not look at him. Instead she scuffed the toe of her shoe back and forth on the worn carpet. Maybe she could make a hole in it. That would teach Dr. Schumacher.

"She'll have to go to a special class, a Sight Saving Class," he went on. "Lessons are made easier there for children with poor eyesight."

"Not go to school with the others!" Mama wailed, hoping she was not understanding.

Dr. Schumacher switched back to German. He spoke gently, soothingly.

"It is a nice place. She'll like it there. You will, Anna. You'll like it very much," he finished.

From the beginning, he had been drawn to this thorny little girl. Now, guessing at how hard life must have been for her since she started school, he wanted more than ever to be her friend.

All of this was in his voice as he spoke straight to her. He not only tried to reassure her about the special class; he also said, without actually putting it into words, that he, Franz Schumacher, liked her, Anna Solden.

Anna went on scratching her shoe back and forth on the bare place in his carpet. She did not look up or answer. He had become part of the bad dream in which she was caught. She hardly heard what he said.

What she did hear, she did not believe. How could she like school?

In the days that followed, the Soldens were busy settling into their new home. Mama and Gretchen scrubbed and polished, aired and dusted. Papa went over everything in the store, finding out what he had, trying to decide what he needed to order. Since Karl Solden's death the store had been kept running by hired help, but now Papa planned to look after it by himself.

"I think he's worried about it," Rudi told the others.

Anna thought so too. Her father seemed to have no minutes to spare, no special smiles to give. She tagged after him, trying to help. Both of them were surprised when she really was a help. She counted cans of peaches, boxes of arrowroot biscuits. She was good at counting. When Papa checked, she was always right. Frieda came too one day; she made mistakes.

"You hurry too much, daughter," Papa said to Frieda.

Anna listened wide-eyed. Could it be that being slow was sometimes a good thing?

Then, three days before school was to begin, Anna's new glasses arrived. Perched on her nub of a nose, they looked like two round moons. She longed to snatch them off and hurl them into a far corner. Instead, she peered through them suspiciously.

For one startled moment, an utterly new expression came over her small plain face, a look of intense surprise and wonder. She was seeing a world she had never guessed existed.

"Oh, Anna, you look just like an owl," Frieda laughed, not meaning any harm.

The wonder left Anna's face instantly. She turned away from her family and stumped off up the stairs to her alcove where none of them could follow without permission. Papa, though, came up alone a minute or two later.

"Do you like them, Anna?" he asked quietly.

She almost told him then. She nearly said, "I never knew you had wrinkles around your eyes, Papa. I knew your eyes were blue but I didn't know they were so bright."

But she remembered Frieda's laughing words. How she hated being laughed at!

"Do I *have* to keep wearing them, Papa?" she blurted.

Papa looked sorry for her but he nodded.

"You must wear them all the time and no non-sense," he said firmly.

Anna reddened slightly. It was not right, fooling Papa like this. But she was not ready to share what had happened to her. Even her father might not understand. She could hardly take it in herself.

"All right, Papa," she said, letting the words drag.

Wanting to comfort her, her father put his hand gently on top of her bent head. She squirmed. He let her go.

"Would you like to come back to the store with me?" he asked.

Anna nodded. Then she said in a muffled voice, "I'll be there in a minute. You go on down."

Ernst Solden started to leave. Then he turned back, stooped suddenly, and kissed her.

"Soon you'll get used to them, *Liebling,*" he consoled her. "Wait and see."

Anna felt her blush grow hotter. She was glad that the light in her alcove was dim.

When he had gone, she lifted her right hand and held it up in front of her. She moved her fingers and counted them. Even though the light was poor, she could see all five. She examined her fingernails. They shone faintly and they had little half-moons at the bottom. Then she leaned forward and stared at her red wool blanket. It was all hairy. She could see the hairs, hundreds of them.

Everything, everywhere she turned, looked new, looked different, looked miraculous.

At last, knowing she was safe, Anna smiled.

9 • THE BEGINNING

"Anna, hurry," Mama called.

Anna pulled up her other long brown stocking and hooked it onto the suspenders which hung from a harness that went over her shoulders. She reached for the cotton petticoat Mama had put ready. Already she was too hot. She felt smothered in clothes. First there was the underwear which came down to her knees, then the straps holding up her suspenders, then the hateful, itchy ribbed stockings and now the petticoat.

Mama pushed aside the curtain that hung across the end of Anna's alcove. "Hurry up," she urged again.

Anna put on her white blouse and buttoned it. It gaped open between the buttons.

Mama sighed. "You grow so fast," she said.

Anna sighed too. She would stop growing if she knew how. She felt far too big already. Her heart lightened, though, as she stretched out her hand for her new tunic.

"One new thing each to start school in," Papa had decided.

Always before, they had whole new outfits for the first day of school, but by now they were getting used to things being different.

Gretchen had chosen a yellow blouse which made her fair hair shine like gold. The boys picked corduroy pants. When they got home, they pranced around in them, making them squeak. For once, Rudi was as silly as Fritz. Frieda and Anna got tunics.

"I hate it," Frieda had stormed. "It's dull and awful. Like a uniform!"

"It looks fine on you," Mama had insisted, ignoring the bright, more expensive dresses. "There is a good big hem to let down and it's serge too. It will last forever."

At that, Frieda moaned as though Mama had plunged a knife into her.

Anna loved her tunic, though. She liked running her fingers down the sharp pleats. She even liked the plainness of it. It *was* like a uniform. Anna had always secretly wanted a uniform.

"Sit up," Mama said now, "while I fix your hair."

When it was done, she sent Anna to show herself to Papa.

Anna hurried until she reached the landing. The rest of the way she walked sedately, for she felt special-looking and grand. She presented herself proudly to her father.

Papa looked at her. Anna waited.

"Klara," he called, "what about ribbons for her hair?"

Anna stood as straight as before but the proud feeling inside her crumpled. She knew what Mama would say. Mama arrived and said it.

"Ribbons will not stay on Anna's hair," Mama said grimly. "However I will try again. Gretchen, run and get your new plaid ribbons."

When Dr. Schumacher arrived to take Mama and her to the new school, Anna was ready with a bright bow on each of her thin braids.

"You look lovely, Anna," the doctor smiled.

Anna looked away. She knew better.

"It is so kind of you to take Anna to this school," Mama fussed, getting herself and Anna into their coats.

"Nonsense," Dr. Schumacher said, "I know Miss Williams. I can help with the English, too. It won't take long."

The three of them found nothing to say to each other as they rode along. When they got out in front of the school, Anna marched along between her mother and the doctor. She tried to look as though this were something she did every day, as though her heart were not thudding so hard against her ribs it almost hurt. Franz Schumacher reached down his big warm hand and gathered up her cold little paw. Anna tried to jerk away but he held on. She gulped and went on walking: one foot . . . the other foot. His hand felt just like Papa's. She left her hand where it was and felt braver.

Miss Williams was the first surprise in what was to be a day of surprises.

"It's lovely to have you with us, Anna," she said when Dr. Schumacher drew Anna forward and introduced her and Mama.

The teacher had a low husky voice, not a bit like Frau Schmidt's. And her smile was so honest that even Anna could not doubt she meant it. She was pretty, too. Her hair was as bright as Gretchen's. She looked at Anna almost the way Papa did.

She doesn't know me yet, Anna reminded herself, not smiling in return. She hasn't heard me read.

"I've brought you a real challenge this time, Eileen," Dr. Schumacher said in an undertone.

Challenge.

Anna did not know that word. Did it mean "stupid one"? But no, it couldn't. Franz Schumacher still had her hand in his and the kindness of his grasp had not changed as he said it. Anna kept the new word in her mind. When she got home, she would ask Papa.

Fifteen minutes later she sat in her new desk and

watched her mother and Dr. Schumacher leave the classroom.

"Don't leave me!" Anna almost cried out after them, her courage deserting her.

Instead, she put one hand up to feel the crispness of Gretchen's hair ribbon. One of the bows was gone. Anna pulled off the other one and shoved it out of sight into the desk.

She must not cry. She must *not*!

Then the desk itself caught her attention and distracted her. She had never seen one like it before. It had hinges on the sides and you could tip it up so that your book was close to you. She looked around wonderingly. The desk was not the only thing that was different. The pencil in the trough was bigger around than her thumb. The blackboards weren't black at all —they were green; and the chalk was fat too, and yellow instead of white.

Even the children were different. Most of them were older than Anna.

"We have Grades One to Seven in this room," Miss Williams had explained to Mama.

The desks were not set in straight rows nailed to the floor. They were pushed into separate groups. Miss Williams put Anna in one right beside her own desk near the front.

"You can sit next to Benjamin," she said. "Ben's been needing someone to keep him on his toes, haven't you, Ben?"

Anna had no idea how she was supposed to keep

Benjamin on his toes. She looked sideways at his feet. They seemed perfectly ordinary.

Was it a joke, maybe?

Anna did not smile. It did not sound like a joke to her.

Quickly, Miss Williams told the new girl the names of all the other children in the class: Jane, Mavis, Kenneth, Bernard, Isobel, Jimmy, Veronica, Josie, Charles. The names flew around Anna's ears like birds, each escaping just as she thought she had it safely captured.

"You won't remember most of them now," the teacher said, seeing panic in the child's eyes. "You'll have to get to know us bit by bit. Bernard is the oldest, so you'll soon know him because he runs us all."

Like Rudi, Anna said to herself. She would keep out of Bernard's way, if she could. Only she wasn't sure which one he was.

"I think you and Ben will probably be working together," Miss Williams went on.

"Introduce her to Ben properly, Miss Williams," a tall boy, who might be Bernard, suggested.

"Anna, allow me to present Benjamin Nathaniel Goodenough," Miss Williams obliged.

Anna stared at the small boy with black tufty hair and an impish face. He was a good head shorter than she was, though his glasses were as big as hers. Behind them, his eyes sparkled.

"I'm named after both my grandfathers," he explained.

"Now you know us well enough to begin with," the teacher said. "It's time we got some work done in this room."

Anna, who had been relaxed studying Benjamin Nathaniel, froze. What now? Would she have to read? She sat as still as a trapped animal while Miss Williams went to a corner cupboard. In a moment, she was back.

"Here are some crayons, Anna," she said. "I'd like you to draw a picture. Anything you like. I'll get the others started and then I'll be free to find out where you are in your schoolwork."

Anna did not take the crayons. She did not know anything she could draw. She was nowhere in her schoolwork. She wanted Papa desperately.

And what did "challenge" mean?

"Draw your family, Anna," Miss Williams said.

She spoke with great gentleness but firmly too, as though she knew, better than Anna did, what the girl could do. She picked up one of Anna's square, stubby hands and closed Anna's fingers around the crayon box.

"Draw your father and your mother, your brothers and your sisters—and yourself, too, Anna. I want to see all of you."

The feel of the box, solid and real, brought back Anna's courage. The crayons were big and bright. They looked inviting. The teacher put paper on the desk, rough, cream-colored paper. Lovely paper for drawing. Six pieces, at least!

"Take your time," Miss Williams said, moving away. "Use as much paper as you need."

Anna took a deep breath. Then slowly she picked out a crayon. She knew how to start, anyway.

She would begin with Papa.

10 • A CHALLENGE

Anna made Papa extra tall. The top of his head touched the edge of the paper. She gave him wide shoulders and a big smile. She made his eyes very blue.

Then she put Mama next to him, holding his arm. Mama came up to his shoulder. Papa often joked about how small Mama was. He could rest his chin on top of her head.

Anna gave Mama a smile too but her crayon slipped as she did it and Mama's smile was crooked. Anna tried to fix it. She scratched at the wax with her fingernail. It flaked off but it left a smeary mark.

Should she start all over again—or give up?

Anna looked down at Papa, so tall, so happy. She drew a new smile on Mama's face over the place where the crooked one had been. This time the smile was fine but you could still see where she had made the mistake.

I know, Anna thought with sudden excitement. I'll make her sunburned and cover it up.

Carefully, she colored in the rest of Mama's face till it was rosy right up to her hair. It worked.

They've been on a holiday, Anna told herself, smiling a little at last. She made Papa's face match.

She paused and thought. By now she had forgotten the rest of the class. Her eyes lighted and she bent over her drawing once more.

She put Fritz's pail in Papa's hand. It didn't show, but Anna knew there was a little fish inside that pail.

Next she put in Rudi and Gretchen. They, too, were tall and sunburned. They had bright yellow hair and bright blue eyes. They had bathing suits on. Rudi was carrying his butterfly net. It was new and he was proud of it. Gretchen had Frieda's pail, full of seashells. The two of them were walking along beside Papa.

The twins took up most of the space next to Mama. They were running, their legs kicking up. Fritz's ears stuck out like cup handles. They both looked much too lively to be carrying their own pails. Anna left them in bare feet.

She colored light brown sand in a band at the bottom of the page.

There. It's done, she told the part of herself that was just watching.

Then she remembered. "And yourself, too, Anna," Miss Williams had said.

There was still a little room left on the page at one side. She made herself fit into the small space. She made her hair plain brown, her eyes an ordinary blue. Wanting somehow to look as interesting as the rest, she tried to draw herself in her new tunic. But she could not make the pleats look like pleats. When she had done her best, the girl on the paper looked squinched up and ugly.

I've spoiled it, mourned Anna. She closed the crayon box.

Miss Williams came and bent above her.

"Who are they, Anna?" she asked.

Slowly Anna began to explain in German.

Miss Williams did not stop her and tell her to talk English instead, but when Anna pointed and said *"Mein Papa,"* the teacher answered "Your father. My, he is tall, isn't he?"

"Yes," Anna replied in English, only half aware she was switching. She was too intent on making sure Miss Williams understood about the holiday.

"They are gone on . . . to the sea," she fumbled, looking in vain for an English word for "holiday."

"I thought they had," Miss Williams said.

It was not such a terrible day. Not once did the teacher ask Anna to read from a book. She printed the story of Anna's picture on another piece of paper. The letters were large and black. Anna read each line as it appeared. She did not panic. She did not think of this as reading.

Here is Anna's father.
He is big. He is happy.
Anna's mother is here too.
She is small. She is happy too.
They are at the sea.
Gretchen is Anna's big sister.
Rudi is Anna's big brother.
Gretchen and Rudi
are happy at the sea.
Frieda is Anna's other sister.
Fritz is Anna's brother too.
Fritz and Frieda are twins.
The twins are happy here too.
Anna is in our class.
Our class is happy
Anna is here.

"You like drawing, don't you, Anna," Miss Williams said, picking up the picture and looking at it again, smiling at the bright colors, the liveliness of the twins.

Anna did not answer. She was too startled, even if she had known what to say. She had always hated drawing in school. Frau Schmidt would put a picture of a tulip up on the board for them to draw. Once, as a special treat, she had brought real flowers in a vase. The others had been pleased with their pictures that day, but in Anna's, the flowers had looked like cabbages on sticks.

"Really, Anna!" Frau Schmidt had said.

Making this portrait of her family, Anna had forgotten that. This had not seemed the same thing at all.

She was still sitting with her mouth ajar when Miss Williams went on to say something else, something so much more surprising that Anna had to pinch herself to make sure she was not inventing the whole thing.

"You like reading, too. I can see that. And your English! I can hardly believe you've been in Canada such a short time. You are amazing, Anna."

Miss Williams was not nearly as amazed as Anna Elisabeth Solden. She, Anna, like reading!

She wanted to laugh but she did not. She still did not even smile openly.

All the same, Anna felt something happening deep inside herself, something warm and alive. She was happy.

She was also muddled. She did not know how to behave. She had never felt this way before, not in school anyway. She sat perfectly still, her plain face as stern as usual. Only her eyes, blinking behind the big new glasses, betrayed her uncertainty.

The teacher did not wait for an answer to the astonishing things she had said. She took the picture and the story and tacked them up on the bulletin board where the whole class could see them. Then she got Benjamin to come over and read the words aloud.

"Twins!" Ben said, his eyes sparkling with interest. "Wow!"

Anna sat and listened to other classes working. She learned about explorers with the boys and girls in Grade Five. Miss Williams did not seem to mind other children listening and learning.

After lunch the teacher wound up the Gramophone and put on a record.

"Get comfortable, everybody," she said, "so you can really hear this."

Another strange word! Anna waited and watched.

Ben sat on the floor, leaning his back against Miss Williams' desk. The boy Anna thought might be Bernard slid down in his seat till all you could see was his head. Mavis put her head down on her folded arms. Everybody relaxed, sprawled, slouched, leaned.

Anna settled herself a little more squarely on her chair. She did not slump or get down on the floor.

But I am comfortable, she told herself.

She stopped worrying about losing Gretchen's hair ribbon, about Miss Williams finding out how stupid she was at schoolwork. She listened with her whole self.

Music, cool quiet music, rippled through the room.

"What did this make you think of?" Miss Williams asked when the record finished.

"Rain," Isobel said. She was in Grade Four and had fat bouncy ringlets.

"I think water maybe," Ben tried.

"Rain's water," Isobel grinned at him.

"No, I mean water like a stream," Ben insisted, staying serious in spite of her.

"What do you think, Anna?" Miss Williams asked. Anna blushed. She had not been going to say.

"I know that music from my home," she explained. "I know the name."

"Tell us," Miss Williams smiled.

"It is 'The Shine of the Moon,'" Anna stumbled. "But . . ."

She stopped short. Miss Williams waited. The others waited too. All the faces turned toward Anna were friendly faces. She took a deep breath and finished.

"I think it is like rain too," she said.

"The record is 'The Moonlight Sonata' by Beethoven," Miss Williams said. "But Beethoven did not name it that. He could have been thinking of rain."

"Or a stream," Ben said stubbornly.

"Or a stream—or something else entirely," the teacher said. "Each of you, listening, will hear it differently. That's fine. That's what your imaginations are for—to use. Beethoven was a great composer. He was German—like Anna."

Anna held her head up at that. She and Beethoven!

Arithmetic was not hard. Numbers, in this classroom, were big and clear and they stayed still when you looked at them.

"Good work, Anna," Miss Williams said, looking over her shoulder.

Not, "Nobody would ever guess you were Gretchen Solden's sister!"

She doesn't even know Gretchen, Anna realized suddenly. She doesn't know any of them but me.

She felt lost for a moment. Her teachers had always known her family too. Then she sat straighter.

Just me, she told herself again.

Whatever this teacher thought of her, it would be because of what she, Anna, did or failed to do. It was a startling idea. Anna was not sure she liked it. She shoved it away in the back of her mind and went on with her arithmetic. But she did not forget.

When school was over, she walked past her own house and went on to the store where Papa was hard at work. She waited off to one side. When the customers were gone, she stepped up and leaned on the counter.

"How did it go in school, my little one?" he asked hopefully.

Anna knew what he hoped but she ignored his question.

"Papa, what is a challenge?" She had said the word over and over to herself all day long so she would be able to ask.

Papa scratched his head.

"A challenge," he repeated. "Well, it is . . . something to be won, maybe. Something special that makes you try hard to win it."

Anna thought that over.

"Thank you, Papa," she said, turning away.

"But school," her father cried after her. "Tell me about it."

"It was fine," Anna said over her shoulder. Then she twirled around unexpectedly and gave him one of her rare half-smiles.

"It was a challenge," she said.

"Something special," she repeated, as she started for home. "Dr. Schumacher thinks I am something special . . . like Papa said. . . . But why something to be won?"

She gave a little hop all at once. She would not mind going back tomorrow.

"It is a challenge," she said over again, aloud, in English, to the empty street.

She liked that word.

11 • THE SECOND DAY

Anna watched her feet walking along.

One . . . two . . . one . . . two . . .

Soon she would be at the school. Maybe she could even see it now if she looked up. She did not look up.

It was a long walk but there was no way to get lost. You just kept going straight ahead after you got to the first big street and turned left. Mama had watched until Anna had made that first turn safely. So she was not lost.

She felt lost though.

One . . . two . . . one . . . two . . .

Yesterday at school they had been nice but she was

new yesterday. Today she would probably be Awkward Anna again. Miss Williams would not smile.

Today she'll want me to read from a book, Anna told herself, getting ready for the worst.

"Hi, Anna," a boy's voice called.

Anna looked up without stopping to think. The next instant, she felt silly. Nobody knew her. There must be another Anna. She glanced around quickly. There were no other girls in sight. Only a tall boy coming along the sidewalk from the opposite direction.

Anna dropped her gaze hastily and quickened her steps. She was almost sure he had been looking right at her and smiling but her new glasses must be playing tricks. She did not know that boy.

They met where the walk led into the school building.

"What's the matter? You deaf?" the boy asked.

He was laughing a little.

Anna darted another glance up at him and then stared at her shoes again.

It's Bernard, she thought, feeling sick.

She was not positive, but she had better answer. Bernard was Rudi's size exactly.

"I am not deaf," she told him.

Her voice was thin and small.

"Good," the boy said. "Hey, why don't you look at me."

Obediently, Anna lifted her head. He was still laughing. Sometimes when Rudi teased, he laughed too.

"That's better," the boy said. "Now I'm going to do you a favor."

Anna had no idea what he was talking about. She was certain now, though, that he was Bernard. She longed to run but something firm in the way he spoke to her made her stay facing him, waiting.

"This will be your first lesson in being a good Canadian," he went on.

"Lesson?" Anna repeated like a parrot.

Her voice was a little stronger now.

"Yeah, lesson. When you hear somebody say 'Hi, Anna,' the way I did, you say 'Hi' back again."

He paused. Anna stared up at him.

"You say 'Hi, Bernard!' " he prompted.

Anna just stood, still not understanding, still not quite brave enough to run.

"Come on or we're both going to be late," he urged. "Just say 'Hi, Bernard.' That's not so hard to say, is it?"

"Hi," Anna heard herself whisper.

She could not manage to add his name. What did "Hi" mean anyway?

Bernard grinned.

"That's a start," he said. "See you in class, kid."

He loped up the walk, leaving her behind. Anna followed slowly.

Somehow she had done the right thing. Bernard had not been mean. But what had it all been about?

She was so puzzled that she was inside the school before she remembered how afraid she was.

Then the nightmare began. She could not find the right classroom. She wandered up one long hall, down another. Through open doorways, she caught sight of groups of children but she recognized nobody. Several boys and girls hurried past her. They all knew exactly where they were going. If one had stopped long enough, she might have been able to ask the way but nobody seemed to see her.

A bell clanged. Anna jumped. Then everywhere the doors were closed.

She went on walking past the tall shut doors. She tried not to think of Papa. She tried not to think at all. She just walked and walked and walked.

"Anna! Anna! This way!"

Footsteps clattered after her. Angel footsteps! But the angel was Isobel, her ringlets bouncing, her eyes warm with sympathy.

"Bernard said he'd seen you so we guessed you must be lost," she explained.

She grabbed Anna's cold hand and squeezed it.

"I know exactly how you feel," she told the new girl, tugging her along, not seeming to mind that Anna could not speak a word in return. "I got lost six times my first week here. This school is so big and all the halls look the same. At recess, I'll show you a sure way to remember. You just have to come in the right door, climb two sets of stairs, turn right and you're there. Here, I mean," she finished.

Before them, like a miracle, was the right door. It

stood open. Nobody was working. Benjamin wasn't even in his desk. He was at the door watching for them. In an instant, Miss Williams was there too.

"Oh, Anna, I'm sorry I wasn't there to meet you," she said.

Anna let Isobel lead her to her desk. She sank into her seat. She listened. Apparently everyone in the class had been lost at least once in the school building. Nobody blamed Anna. Not once did anyone say, "How stupid of you not to have paid better attention yesterday!"

"I got lost once just coming back from the bathroom," Ben said and blushed.

The rest laughed. Ben didn't seem to mind. He smiled himself.

"I expect you were daydreaming, Ben," Miss Williams commented.

"I was figuring out whether a person could dig a tunnel under the Atlantic Ocean," Benjamin admitted.

The class laughed again. Anna stopped trembling. Here in Canada, she thought, maybe it is all right to make mistakes.

"Now it's time we stopped gossiping," Miss Williams told them. "Take your place, Ben."

Ben went to his desk. Miss Williams moved to stand at the front of the room. As she opened her mouth to begin, a voice spoke up.

"Hi, Anna," Bernard said.

Anna looked at him. Then she looked at the teacher.

Miss Williams was smiling, waiting. Anna gripped the edge of her desk.

"Hi, Bernard," she said, still in a whisper.

"I'm teaching her to be a Canadian," Bernard explained.

Miss Williams did not look surprised.

"Good," she said simply. "Class, stand."

When it was time for recess, Isobel did not forget. Ben came along too. They took Anna to the door through which she would enter the school.

"It's the door you'd come to naturally, walking from your place," Isobel said.

Anna's surprise showed on her face. How did Isobel know where the Soldens lived?

"I heard Dr. Schumacher tell Miss Williams your address yesterday," Isobel confessed. "I live on the same street, two blocks this way. Now listen, you come in here . . ."

"Cross-eyed . . . cross-eyed!" a voice in the playground sang out.

Anna did not know what the words meant. Until she saw her stiffen, she did not know they had anything to do with Isobel.

"Ignore them, Isobel," Ben urged. "Pretend you don't even hear, like Miss Williams said."

"Four-eyes . . . four-eyes!" another voice took up the mocking chant.

Isobel let the school door close, shutting the three of them safely inside. She smiled shakily at Ben.

"Ignore them yourself, Benjamin," she advised.

"I hate them!" Ben said, through clenched teeth.

"Me too . . . but hating doesn't help," Isobel said. "It would if we were a lot bigger."

She caught the bewilderment on Anna's face.

"She doesn't know what they mean," she said to Ben.

She explained about crossed eyes. Anna did not get all the words but she understood the gestures. Isobel's eyes did cross sometimes but they were nice eyes, brown and kind. Anna remembered the brightness in them that morning when Isobel had found her. She, like Ben, hated whoever called Isobel names.

"Four-eyes" meant glasses. Ben pointed to his eyes and then to each of his round lenses, counting them up.

"Four," he finished.

Anna looked at his earnest face. She hesitated. Could she make herself understood? Then she tried.

"Maybe I was it," she told him.

Ben looked at Isobel for help.

"What did you say?" Isobel asked Anna.

That hateful English! She should have known better than to attempt it. Then in a flash, Anna knew what to do. She imitated Ben, pointing to her own eyes and lenses as she counted.

"Ohhhh," Ben and Isobel said together. They laughed, the tension leaving their faces.

"Join the crowd," Isobel said.

As she spoke, she put her arm around Anna's shoulders and hugged her quickly, lightly.

"Come on. We're showing her how to find the room," Ben reminded them.

Anna followed her guides. She did not know what "join the crowd" meant exactly, but she was suddenly glad she had tried out her English.

Then, as she climbed the stairs with the other two, she remembered the tormenting singsong voices outside and she scowled. So there were boys like Rudi in Canada too. She had been wrong about Bernard, but there were others.

She had been very wrong about Bernard. He spoke to her again that afternoon when school was over and he was about to leave.

"So long, Anna," he said.

Anna did not know it but she reminded Bernard of a stray cat. He had rescued so many stray cats that his mother had refused to let him in the door with one ever again. Now he waited for Anna to answer him. He did not hurry her. You had to be gentle and patient with strays.

At last Anna responded.

"So long?" she said, making a question out of it.

"It just means 'Good-bye till later,'" the boy explained. She understood—it meant *"Auf wiedersehen."*

He smiled at her and left, forgetting her the moment she was out of sight.

Anna did not forget. All the way to Papa's store, she thought and thought about Bernard.

A bell chimed when she opened the door. Anna listened for it. It was as though the store said "Hi, Anna."

It is a Canadian store, she thought.

Papa was busy. Anna did not mind. She drifted back to a shadowy corner and perched on an upended orange crate. Already she had chosen this dim room, so crowded with things and yet so peaceful, as a refuge. Even Papa did not have a lot of time to notice her here. Sometimes it was nice not being noticed. Sometimes you had things to think about, private things.

She could see Papa weighing some cheese for a plump lady. She watched him count oranges into a bag. But she was not thinking about him.

"Hi, Bernard," whispered Anna. "So long, Bernard."

Now Papa was climbing up a set of steps to get down a mousetrap.

I could say it to the others too maybe, Anna thought. Hi, Isobel. So long, Ben.

She gasped at her own daring. Yet one of these days, she might.

The stout lady said, "Thank you, Mr. Solden," and went out.

Isobel put her arm around me, remembered Anna.

Papa was the only person who hugged her. When anyone else tried, she went stiff and jerked away. She could not help it. Sometimes she did not even want to. But she still did.

"Anna's not a loving child," Mama had said once to

Aunt Tania when Anna had squirmed away from a kiss.

But today, with Isobel, it had been different.

No fuss, thought Anna. Just nice.

Papa had turned. He was peering through the shadows, looking for her. Anna waited for him to find her in her corner. They smiled at each other across the store.

"Good afternoon, Anna," her father said.

She looked at him. In all her world, he was the kindest person. He would not laugh at her even if she got it wrong. Papa never laughed at her when he knew she was serious. She took a deep breath.

"Hi, Papa," said Anna in a loud, brave voice.

It sounded fine.

12 • A DIFFERENT DIRECTION

Now Anna set off in a different direction from the others every morning and got home later than they did at night. She said very little about school and that little only when she was asked outright.

"What is it like, this class of yours?" Mama wanted to know.

"It's all right," said Anna.

Mama threw up her hands in despair.

"It is like trying to get water out of a stone," she complained.

"Can you read yet, Anna?" Frieda asked.

Anna ducked her head so that her sister could not see her face.

"Some," she said.

She can't, Frieda thought, and she wished she had not asked.

The first week was over. Then the next. Still Anna's family had no idea what was happening to her at school. They were not surprised. They were used to Anna and her moods, Anna and her silences. They hoped for the best.

Papa saw more of her than the others because she came to the store almost every afternoon. He had work to do, so he could not spend time drawing her out. But one afternoon he heard her singing to herself. He went on stacking cans of soup with his back to her.

"O Canada, my home and native land," Anna practiced softly.

Papa nearly dropped a tin. What was happening to his Anna?

Bernard was helping. Ben was certainly part of it. Isobel, who still kept Anna under her wing, made some of the difference. But mostly it was Miss Williams who sought and began to find a new Anna.

It was not easy. It took weeks.

"Well done, Anna!" the teacher said whenever she honestly could. One day she added, "How quick you are!"

Anna thought, the first time, that Miss Williams had mixed her up with some other child. Everyone knew that Awkward Anna was slow, slow, slow. When the teacher said it again, though, Anna realized the truth. Now that her glasses made letters and numbers sharp and easy to tell apart, now that she could see what was printed on the board, she, Anna, was quick. Sometimes she was even quicker than Ben.

She sat exulting over her first perfect arithmetic paper. Suddenly she heard Miss Williams say softly, "Anna, what a pretty smile you have."

Anna's smile vanished. The girl waited for the next words, words like, "Why don't you smile more often instead of looking so sulky?" But Miss Williams turned to Isobel and began explaining what was wrong with her long division. She did not seem to think she had said anything surprising.

Anna practiced smiling after that. To start with, she did it shyly and seldom. Yet Miss Williams always smiled back, and before she knew it, the other children were smiling at her too. Ben's grin was so catching Anna could not help answering with one of her own. Her smiles still did not last long but they came more and more often.

"I wish I had dimples like yours, Anna Solden," Miss Williams sighed. Anyone could tell it was a sigh of real envy. "I've always longed for a dimple."

Anna did not know she had dimples. She did not know what dimples were. When Isobel explained, Anna poked the tip of her finger into the one in her right cheek. She smiled; it was there. She stopped smiling; it was gone. Swiftly, gaily, it came and went. Anna blushed faintly.

And I have two of them, she thought.

That night, at supper, she watched Frieda and Gretchen. At last Frieda laughed at one of Fritz's jokes. Then Gretchen smiled too. Neither of them had even one dimple.

Then, halfway through October, Miss Williams came to Anna's desk one morning with a book in her hands.

"I have a present for you, Anna," she said. "It's yours to keep. Much of it is too hard for you to read yet but I think you will like it anyway. It will be a challenge for you."

At the word "challenge," Anna's face lighted. She took the book into her own hands. On the cover there was a picture of a tall gate. Through the bars, she could see two children in a garden.

"*A . . . Ch . . . Chil . . .*" she began slowly, frowning over the words.

"Child's," the teacher helped her.

"*A Child's Garden of . . . Verses*," Anna said triumphantly. "What is 'verses'?"

"Poems," Ben told her. "Look."

He reached for the book, opened it and showed her.

"Ohhh, *Gedichte*," Anna said, understanding.

"The man who wrote the poems had no brothers and sisters," the teacher said, pulling up a chair and sitting down next to Anna's desk. "His name was Robert Louis Stevenson."

"Didn't he write the one about the swing?" Jane asked.

Miss Williams nodded and smiled at Jane. She went on as though she were telling them a story. The whole class listened.

"He was sick a lot. All his life really. And I think he was often very lonely when he was little. He played lots of games with his imagination, though."

Imagination was a long word but Anna knew what it meant. Miss Williams loved imagination. Just the day before she had looked at one of Anna's drawings of a giant striding out of his castle with his head above the clouds and she had said, "You have a fine imagination, Anna." Anna had never thought before about what kind of imagination she had but she could not doubt Miss Williams. Imagination was one thing Miss Williams knew all about.

Does Gretchen have a fine imagination? Anna wondered. She thought not.

Now she opened her book and began to leaf through the pages. The teacher went away and left her.

"Try these problems, Ben," she said. Ben got busy. Miss Williams started the four children in Grade Three hearing each other practice their multiplication tables.

Nobody bothered Anna. Nobody told her to put the book away or asked her to stand and read from it. All morning long she was left with her present, left to puzzle over it and discover its treasures for herself.

Much of it *was* too hard for her. But the very first poem she tried to read, she understood. It was about getting up in the dark in winter and having to go to bed while it was still light during the summer. Mama was strict about bedtime. Anna knew exactly how Robert Louis Stevenson felt. She read the last verse over again, nodding her head.

> And does it not seem hard to you,
> When all the sky is clear and blue,
> And I should like so much to play,
> To have to go to bed by day?

She found another one though, that morning, which was forever after her favorite. It was called "The Lamplighter."

Isobel was not certain what a lamplighter was so Miss Williams had to come to their rescue. She described the gas lamps which had lined the street when Stevenson was a child and told them about the lamplighter—the man who came and lighted them every evening.

"I love that poem too, Anna," she said with a smile as she went back to help Grade Six with geography.

Anna read the middle verse over.

> Now Tom would be a driver and Maria go to sea,
> And my papa's a banker and as rich as he can be;
> But I, when I am stronger and can choose what I'm to do,
> O Leerie, I'll go round at night and light the lamps with you.

"Who were Tom and Maria?" she asked, interrupting geography.

Miss Williams did not tell her it was rude to interrupt. "Maybe his cousins," she said. "He played with them sometimes."

Anna smiled over Maria wanting to go to sea. She thought of asking Miss Williams if Mr. Stevenson had ever become a lamplighter. Somehow, she did not need to ask. He had written poems instead.

She went on to the part she liked best:

And oh! before you hurry by with ladder and with light,
O Leerie, see a little child and nod to him tonight!

She waited, this time, for the teacher to notice her. Miss Williams seemed to feel her waiting.

"Yes, Anna?" she asked.

"Do you think Leerie *did* see him there, Miss Williams?" Anna's heart was in the words.

"Yes, I do," Miss Williams said simply. "I think that is what made Mr. Stevenson remember him all those years later. May I read it to the others?"

Anna held out the book.

"Perhaps you would help me," the teacher said. "Could you read the last verse, do you think?"

Anna had never been invited to read aloud before. Frau Schmidt had given orders, not invitations.

"I'll help if you get stuck," Miss Williams assured her, and began:

*"My tea is nearly ready and the sun has left the sky.
It's time to take the window to see Leerie going by;"*

Everyone was listening, even the boy and girl in Grade Seven.

"All right, Anna," Miss Williams said. Anna gulped and started to read the last verse. She had read it over several times. She hardly stumbled.

*"For we are very . . . lucky, with a lamp before the door, . . .
And Leerie . . . stops to light it . . . as he lights so many . . . more, . . ."*

Two more lines and it was done. Miss Williams had not had to help once. Anna looked up, her face shining.

"Good for you, Anna," said Miss Williams.

At noon, Anna went up to the teacher's desk, the book in her hands.

"Is this really my own book?" she asked, unable to believe in the gift.

"Your very own. You may take it home."

"I told you so, Anna," Ben reminded her. "She gives everybody a book. She gave me *The Wizard of Oz.*"

"Thank you," Anna said.

She should have said that right away, she realized. Embarrassment made the words sound stiff and formal. Yet the teacher smiled.

Then she stopped smiling. Anna was putting the book back inside her desk.

"Anna, I said you might take it home," she repeated.

Anna turned. Her face was wooden.

"Cannot I leave it here?"

"Wouldn't you rather take it home?" the teacher asked.

"No," Anna said.

"All right. You may do whatever you like with it. It's your book," Miss Williams assured her.

Again she wondered what was wrong at Anna's home. She had asked Franz Schumacher about the Soldens, but he had been puzzled too.

"They seem a happy family except for Anna," he had said. "She's the youngest, of course, but that shouldn't make her so . . . so bristly. Perhaps it started when nobody understood she had trouble seeing."

Anna marched out of the classroom to go home for lunch. The new book waited in her desk. Miss Williams waited too. Was she going to have to begin all over again to win Anna's slow trust, to coax from her that shy smile?

But when Anna came back, her prickles were gone. She hurried to her place, her face eager and alive. Immediately she got out her new book.

First she reread the poems she had mastered that morning. Then she started on a new one. It was harder. She could not even read the title. She sounded out the words slowly, moving her lips, whispering the syllables aloud.

" 'Es . . . cape . . . at . . . Bed . . . time.' "

She turned to Isobel for help but only a little help. She wanted to read it herself.

The book was so lovely, the poems like music, the pictures wonderful. And it was a challenge.

"Like me," Anna Solden told herself with satisfaction.

13 • AFTER SCHOOL

Toward the end of October Papa began to need help at the store, yet he could not afford to hire anyone. One night he came home too tired to eat. He slumped forward, his head on his hands, and when Mama brought him his plate, he pushed it away, saying only, "Not now, Klara. I just can't."

That was when Mama spoke up.

"I know what you need," she commented, dropping into the chair across from him.

"What?" Papa said wearily, not even looking up.

Mama hesitated for a moment. It was not like her to stop short of saying what she meant to say. The children were finishing their dessert. All five looked around at her, even if Papa did not. Mama seemed unusually pink and was she flustered? Fritz poked Frieda with his toe. Frieda jabbed him back, agreeing that something was up.

Mama cleared her throat. Anna saw her hands twist together in her lap.

"Yes, Klara?" Papa said. He, too, was curious now. "What do I need?"

"Me," Mama said.

The one word popped out like a cork coming out of a bottle. Other words rushed after it. She explained how she could help. The store needed cleaning. She had seen that for a long time. And she knew just how to display the vegetables. And she had been at the head of her class in bookkeeping. Of course, that had been years ago and she knew things had changed and maybe he did not want her. He just had to say so. She would understand. But all the children were in school and she knew nobody here and she had nothing to do . . .

Anna stared in fascination at her mother. She was sure Mama had not yet taken a breath. If she did not run down soon, she might explode.

Papa stood up. He strode around the table. He leaned down and kissed his wife soundly, stopping the flood of words.

"You will be a gift from heaven," he said.

Mama began the very next day. After school Anna

went to the store as usual. Papa, hearing the door chime, turned, saw her, and smiled broadly.

"Your mother is a better storekeeper than I am," he boasted. "Look around. You will see how clever she is."

Anna looked. He was right. Already the place was brighter. Mama had put in stronger light bulbs. There were no truly dim corners left. A lot of the dust had vanished too.

Anna stood watching. Mama noticed her.

"Don't block the doorway, child," she said.

When customers came, Klara Solden acted as though she had always been there. Her English was still strange but she launched into it anyway, advising ladies about bargains, assuring them that the eggs were fresh.

Once when she meant "fresh," she said "raw." The lady she said it to laughed at her.

"Well, I didn't intend to buy cooked eggs," she said.

Mama tried to correct her mistake but got flustered and could not think of the word she wanted. The lady turned away, as though Anna's mother was not even there, and started poking at the fruit, turning apples over and putting them back.

I know how you feel, Mama, Anna thought. I know exactly.

If her mother had not started to talk with someone else, the girl might have gone to her then and there and spilled out her secret. At home she still spoke

German but at school she now talked English all the time. Well, almost. Soon she planned to tell them at home. She daydreamed about how amazed they were going to be. But not yet. First she wanted her English to be perfect. She did not want Rudi to catch her making even the smallest mistake.

"Anna, don't upset those cans," Mama called over at her.

Anna shook her head to say she would not. Then she went home. The store was no longer her place. Not only the dust had disappeared. The quiet was gone too. Without the dust and the dimness, without the peace, without the chance to have Papa to herself for minutes at a time, Anna saw no reason to stay.

The next afternoon, she dawdled when school was let out. She was in no hurry to get home. She was still too young to play with the others, new glasses or no new glasses. Sometimes now she watched and thought she might be able to do the things they did if they would only ask her. They did not understand how changed her world was. They did not think to ask.

"Anna, aren't you going to the store?" Isobel puffed, catching up to her as she went down the street like a snail.

Trudging along, looking at her feet, Anna shook her head.

"We can walk together then," said Isobel.

Anna's unhappiness was still wrapped around her like a thick cloak. She did not really hear Isobel's words for a moment. She made no response and Isobel stepped back.

"Forget it," she said, her eyes still puzzled. "I thought you'd want to."

Then Anna understood. Almost too late, she threw off her misery. Her face glowed.

"I do want to, Isobel," she said. "It would be very nice."

Isobel was not bothered by the stilted words. She knew Anna. From then on they walked together almost every day. Now that Anna was so busy listening to Isobel's constant chatter, she had little time to worry about missing going to the store. The older girl knew everything. She told Anna about Ben's father who played a violin in an orchestra and sometimes waited on tables. She explained what Halloween was. She gossiped about Miss Williams.

"I think she's in love," Isobel said.

Anna's mouth dropped open. "You do!" she exclaimed. "Who is she in love with?"

For once, Isobel failed her. "I'm not sure," she said mysteriously, "but I have an idea."

Anna nodded sagely. Isobel just was not telling.

The first time the older girl asked her to come and meet her mother, however, Anna hung back. Even with Isobel along to give her courage, she did not want to go into a strange house and face an unknown adult.

"Oh, come *on*!" Isobel pulled at her arm. "She won't eat you. As a matter of fact, she'll feed you."

Inside the front hall, Anna tried to get behind her friend.

"Mo-*ther!*" Isobel yelled, shattering the silence.

Then Mrs. Brown was there, smiling at Anna with a smile so like Isobel's that the new Anna smiled bravely back.

"Anna, I'm so pleased to meet you," Mrs. Brown said.

Maybe I'm getting better looking, Anna thought as she stood in bashful silence but went on smiling.

No, nothing had changed about her except her new glasses.

And my dimples, Anna remembered.

Somehow she was sure she had not had dimples back in Germany.

"How about some bread and butter and brown sugar?" Mrs. Brown broke in on her thoughts.

Suddenly Anna felt empty right down to her toes.

"Yes, please," she said, as though she had always known Isobel's mother.

The two girls stopped in for a snack almost every day after that. Anna, realizing after a week or two how one-sided this was, asked Papa if she could bring Isobel to the store sometimes for something to eat.

"Of course," Papa said at once. "Any time, Anna."

Mama talked about it a bit more. Anna had known she would. She had never brought a friend to meet them before. She had not had anyone to bring.

"What is she like, this Isobel?" asked Mama. "Is she German?"

"You will see. No, not German," was all Anna would say.

She knew Papa would like Isobel. She thought Mama might not like the way her eyes crossed. But Mrs. Solden smiled at Isobel as warmly as Mrs. Brown had smiled at Anna.

"Here are oatmeal cookies," she said. "Just one each, though."

She put the rest of the box behind the counter especially for them.

"Your mother's nice," Isobel said afterward as they nibbled their cookies to make them last.

Anna took another tiny bite. "Yes," she said, "she is."

She had almost answered, "Not as nice as Papa," but she had caught the words back. They had not seemed fair even if they were how she felt. Mama had given them the cookies.

One afternoon in November as the girls neared the Browns', Isobel said, "When I was little, Mum used to give me a glass of milk with my bread. And she'd always want to know if I wanted more."

Anna was silent, taking this in.

"Then last year, when Dad couldn't get work, she didn't give me anything at all," Isobel went on, her voice low.

Anna thought this over. It was her turn to say something.

"It is the money," she said. "My Mama and Papa, they worry too about the money. Rudi says when he

was small, he could have all the cookies he wanted. But he might be lying."

Isobel nodded. Then, her face brightening, she went on, "But we will have Christmas this year no matter what. Mother promised."

Anna stopped dead in the middle of the sidewalk and stared at her friend.

"Always there is Christmas," she stated.

"Not last year," Isobel said. "Oh, we got one thing each, something to wear. But that was all. Dad said he was sorry but there was just no use in hanging up our stockings. The Depression had hit Santa Claus too, he said."

Anna had to have a lot of this explained to her. She had never hung up a stocking. She quickly understood that Santa Claus was Saint Nicholas, *der Weihnachtsmann*—the Christmas Man. She did not know what the Depression was. Isobel did well with the first two but all she knew about the Depression was that her father had lost his job and there had been no money. Now he had a new job.

"He works for my uncle," Isobel said. "They're undertakers."

"Under . . . what?" Anna asked.

Isobel's cheeks went pink but she smiled.

"That is a word you really should know, Anna Solden," she said. Then she explained. Isobel had to explain many, many things to Anna many times a day.

It was tiring sometimes, but she did not really mind because Anna remembered what she was told. She would mutter each new word to herself, and next thing, you would hear her using it talking to Ben or even Bernard. Isobel, who worshipped Bernard, wished she knew how Anna had become such a friend of his.

"Undertaker," Anna was murmuring now. "Undertaker."

Isobel's eyes sparkled. She hoped she was there when Anna tried to use that word. Anna looked up, caught her laughing, and laughed too. Alone with Isobel, laughter came naturally to the youngest of the Soldens.

That night at supper, Gretchen announced, "Papa, I have to have skates!"

Papa said nothing. Gretchen leaned toward him.

"All the girls skate," she said. "They were talking about it today. When the ice is thick enough, that's all they'll do."

"Wait a little," her father said. "Christmas is coming."

Gretchen thought Christmas was a long way off but she held her tongue. She knew her parents were worried about money. She wished she were Anna's age again. Look at Anna right now! She was positively beaming. Gretchen wanted to slap her.

"Nothing's funny, Anna," she said coldly, "so stop smirking."

"Gretchen," Papa said ominously.

"I'm sorry," Gretchen muttered, wishing she really dared slap her little sister.

Rudi, who had already traded his stamp collection for secondhand skates, gave her a look of sympathy. He knew what was important here in Canada even if none of the others did.

Neither of them guessed that Anna smiled because Papa had just said, "Christmas is coming." They, who knew so much, had never dreamed that Christmas might not come. Anna, after her talk with Isobel, knew it was not certain at all. If there was no money, they would have to do without Christmas.

But now Papa had as good as promised. Gretchen or no Gretchen, Anna smiled on.

She saw her father look at her anxiously. Maybe he thought she, too, wanted skates. But she didn't. Just Christmas itself, with the magic of the tree, with the singing, with special things to eat, special smells in the air, with extra happiness all through the house—that was what made her joyful.

"Enough about skates," Mama said. "Who wants to wash the dishes and be my dearest child?"

She was laughing, teasing them.

"You know something, Klara," Papa said, the tension leaving his face. "I think working in that store all day agrees with you. You are turning back into your old self."

"Maybe, maybe," Mama said. "But I am still looking for a dishwasher."

At last Gretchen volunteered. It was her turn any-way. But lately, when Rudi took the garbage out without being asked, when Frieda sewed on her own button, when Gretchen helped to clean the silver which had finally come from Frankfurt, when Fritz sang his mother German songs, each of them became "the dearest child." Life was getting back to normal. Even Anna liked it.

Not that she had herself become "the dearest child" at home.

"Anna, hurry and get the table set," Mama called the very next night.

Still something in her voice said Anna was slow. Anna, trying to be quick, put the forks and knives crookedly and one spoon upside down.

"Oh, Anna," Mama sighed, as they sat down. "When will you learn to take care!"

Anna straightened her own fork and felt anger boiling up inside her. Hadn't Mama said to hurry? She began to eat in silence, leaning over her soup bowl.

"And don't slouch," Mama went on. "You're so round-shouldered."

She had just told Fritz to eat more quietly but Anna did not notice that.

Always I am the one she picks on, she stormed in-side herself. She did not straighten up.

Fritz too felt picked on. He too thought it was unfair. He looked sideways at Anna's furious face. "At least I speak English," he said virtuously.

That was too much. Anna, who never answered them back when they teased, who stared straight through her tormenters, forgot the cold silence she had mastered under Frau Schmidt and exploded.

"You shut up!" she yelled at Fritz, who could not believe his ears.

"Shut up, shut up, SHUT UP!" she added to make sure he got the message. In English, too!

Then she jumped up and ran from the table up the stairs to her own alcove where she threw herself, face down, on the bed.

This time, nobody would come up after her. In the Solden family, nobody ever left the table without being excused first by Papa. She had just been ruder than she had ever been in her life before.

And she had enjoyed it. She giggled into her pillow, remembering how Fritz's eyes had popped. Then she stopped and lay very still. Was Papa terribly angry?

If she had gone to the stairs and listened, she would have heard her father telling the family that they were to stop teasing Anna and tormenting her.

"I've told you and told you that she is the youngest. And she does speak some English, Fritz, with that friend of hers. I've heard her. At home, we could all talk German now sometimes. We do not want to lose our own language."

Anna, not hearing, told herself that it did not matter what anyone else thought if only Papa was not too angry.

Then, suddenly, her eyes gleamed and she began to

sing softly, under her breath, at Mama, at Fritz, at the whole world which tried to bother her.

> *And if tyrants take me*
> *And throw me in prison,*
> *My thoughts will burst free*
> *Like blossoms in season.*
> *Foundations will crumble.*
> *The structure will tumble.*
> *And free men will cry,*
> "Die Gedanken sind frei!"

14 • RUDI'S MEETING

Everywhere in Toronto, store windows and colored lights and radio programs and the Santa Claus Parade were telling children that Christmas was coming. Fritz and Frieda had been asked to sing a duet in German at the school Christmas Concert. Rudi had asked for a dog. He asked every year at Christmas, although all the children, Rudi included, knew he would not get one. Mama said five children were enough wild life.

The first snow fell and melted by mid-morning. The second drifted down in fat lazy flakes and stayed on the ground like spun sugar for two whole days.

"Do they have Christmas trees here, Ernst?" Mama asked.

Her eyes twinkled. Anna was certain she was teasing. Still, she felt frightened for a moment till Papa said, "Of course!"

In spite of his sureness, in spite of the snow and the carols and the talk of the puppy they would not get, in spite of everything beginning to point to Christmas, there was an uneasiness in the house. The children tried to pretend it did not exist. After all, Mama and Papa did talk of Christmas—but not in the old way. Always before, they had entered eagerly into the planning. This year, they looked at each other soberly and remained silent.

"Rudi, what's wrong with Papa and Mama?" Fritz put it into words at last.

"I'm not sure," Rudi said slowly.

I know, Anna thought.

She did not tell because Rudi was the oldest. It was up to him to decide such important things. Perhaps, though, Rudi did not have a friend like Isobel who could explain.

It is the Depression, Anna said wisely to herself. It is not enough money.

Gretchen, not Rudi, arrived at the same answer. A couple of days later, when the children were alone in the house, she made it clear.

"People just aren't buying enough at the store,"

she said. "I think they don't have enough money for the kind of Christmas we had in Frankfurt."

As she finished speaking, she gave a sharp sigh. Anna knew her big sister's dream of ice skates was vanishing.

Rudi glowered at her.

"Well, there's nothing we can do about that," he said, throwing himself down into Papa's chair. "We all have to go to school."

"If I were old enough, I'd quit and go to work," Fritz announced.

He sounded so wistful they all laughed. Everyone knew how much Fritz loved school! Without Frieda's help, he would have failed long ago. He was clever but he was lazy too.

"We'd all be glad to stop school, you Dummkopf!" Rudi said.

I wouldn't, Anna thought.

For so long she had dreamed about the heaven of no school. It was queer to know, all at once, how much she would miss it now.

"Everybody think hard tomorrow," Rudi said. "Kids in books always have ideas and save the family from starvation. Get home right after school and we'll compare notes. There must be something!"

When they came down to breakfast the next morning, though, Rudi had had an idea already.

"What is it, Rudi?" Frieda said in a stage whisper while Mama was in the kitchen for a moment. Papa had gone to the store before any of them were downstairs.

"Shhh," he warned her, frowning. Mama was coming back. "Just hurry tonight. I'll tell you then."

Mama, who used to be able to read their very thoughts, seemed unaware of the stir of excitement as the children left for school. When Anna shut the door behind herself, Mama was at the closet getting her coat. Every morning she hurried to the store as soon as they were gone.

Anna tried to think that day but she was busy learning a new poem by heart and showing Ben how to carry when you add. Anyway, Rudi had the answer.

"I can't wait tonight," she gasped at Isobel after school and streaked for home as fast as she could.

She was still late. She had farther to come than the others and the sidewalks were slippery. They would go on without her, of course. All the same, she was breathless when she tugged the front door open.

From the hall, as she struggled out of her scarf and coat, mittens and hood, she listened.

Rudi was in the middle of a speech. She could hear him walking up and down importantly as he talked. Papa did that sometimes.

"So that's what we'll do," he said. "This year, we'll make our presents for them and save them the Christmas money Papa always hands out. When they go to give it to you, Gretchen, you can just say, 'Thank you, but this time we have decided to make our own arrangements.' I'm pretty sure, the more I think about it, that they're worrying about money for Christmas as much as anything. I mean, we can let down our old clothes and stuff. And Mama's more careful about food. So the presents must be the thing. It's good we don't give each other anything."

Everyone talked at once. Anna, tucking her mittens into her coat pocket, smiled. Good for Rudi!

"Great idea!" Fritz didn't know he was agreeing with her.

"I don't need you to tell me what to say to Papa," Gretchen had her nose in the air. Then Anna, from the doorway, saw her grin at her older brother. "You did make it sound grand though," she admitted. "Tell me again."

While Gretchen practiced the words over in an airy unreal voice and Anna leaned over to unbuckle her galoshes, the twins clamored for attention.

"But, Rudi, we're no good at making things."

Anna felt a sudden chill. She worked on the next buckle. It was stiff. What would Rudi say?

"Can you earn money?" Rudi wanted to know.

"Well . . . maybe," Fritz ventured for them both.

"Buy them something then," Rudi lightly brushed aside their anxiety. He was not going to have anyone or anything stand in the way of his plan. "That's what I'm going to do myself."

"How?"

"You'll see. I promise you one thing though. It's

going to be the best present of them all," boasted Rudi.

Anna kicked her overshoes off. The other four turned at the sound and discovered her. She watched, while dismay broke over each face in turn.

"What in the world can Anna give them?" Gretchen was the one who put it into words.

"Oh, she doesn't count. She's only nine," Rudi said too quickly. Staring up at the ceiling, suddenly he started to whistle.

He was wrong about her not counting. With Ben she counted. With Isobel. With Papa. With Miss Williams. Anna knew that. But the words still flicked at her in a way that hurt.

Still, could she make a Christmas present for her parents? Rudi could earn money easily. He said so himself. And Gretchen knitted almost as well as Mama. The twins, Anna was sure, would find a way.

They are full of imagination, she thought.

She alone could do nothing.

Gretchen, still staring at her, suddenly cried out, "Don't you worry, Anna. I'll knit something to be from you. If I start right away, I'll have time, I'm sure."

Before Anna had time to answer, Rudi said roughly, "Oh, Gretel, don't be so silly. They won't expect anything from her once they know we're making the presents ourselves. I think we should try to make them really *great* things."

The Anna Solden who had lived in Frankfurt would

have seen that Rudi was right and given up before she started. But this was another Anna. She was braver now, a little older, and much better at making things. Sometimes, now, she could even see the hole in the needle. She came a step into the room and then another. She still had not spoken but she was thinking harder than she had ever thought before.

Drawings maybe? Miss Williams liked her drawings. She could put some into a sort of book.

But Rudi could draw galloping horses that practically moved across the page and Frieda often sat and sketched Mama while she ironed, or Papa reading a book, and anyone could tell right away who they were supposed to be and what they were doing.

Not pictures, Anna decided.

"You really are mean, Rudi," Gretchen flared. "Of course Anna will want to give something. And I will so knit her something. If it's from Anna, it needn't be anything big or special."

The last sentence jabbed into Anna like the thrust of a knife. Suddenly, she stopped thinking. Her chin shot up. Her eyes, behind her big glasses, sparked with anger and humiliation. They would see. She would show them.

"I will give my own present, thank you very much, Lady Gretchen," she threw the words like darts. "You can keep your stupid old knitting. People only say they like it to make you feel good. Everyone knows it's full of mistakes."

Then, before any of them could come back with a

retort to remind her who she was—the youngest, the *Dummkopf*, Awkward Anna—she wheeled around and left the room.

She headed for the stairs, not caring what they would say, but she heard Rudi whether she wanted to or not.

"I told you, Gretchen," he jeered. "Helping Anna is like trying to pat a biting dog."

Gretchen did not answer though. Anna paused. Still Gretchen did not speak.

All at once, Anna wished she had not said that last bit about the mistakes in Gretchen's knitting; but she did not go back. Her sister deserved it.

"If it's from Anna, it needn't be anything big or special."

Who did Gretchen think she was?

At the top of the stairs, Anna veered and went to look at herself in the bathroom mirror. She was not interested in the sight of her own face. To her, it was dull and plain. She had never seen it when her dimples flashed. But she could talk to herself better sometimes when she could see herself at the same time.

"Can I make a present?" she asked the girl in the mirror. "How can I earn money? A lot of money!" she added recklessly.

She might as well make her wishes big.

But the girl in the mirror looked as discouraged as Anna felt. She hunched up her shoulders, made a face at herself, and turned away.

Papa might help, Anna thought suddenly.

But no.

This present had to be a surprise, a secret. It would not be fair to go to Papa.

Anna wandered into her alcove and lay on her cot. She did not search for an inspiration any longer. She just hoped. Maybe, somehow, something wonderful would happen yet.

Three months before, she would not have hoped at all.

The front door opened and closed. Mama and Papa were home. The youngest of the Soldens got to her feet and started down the stairs. Gretchen had put the meat pie into the oven. It smelled like heaven.

Mama smelled it too. Before she had her coat off, she gave Gretchen a grateful hug.

"So it is you who are the dearest child tonight, my Gretel," she said. "It is so cold out. The hot pie is just what we are needing."

Anna was hungry and the pie was delicious, even if there was not really much meat in it. But she could not finish hers.

"Are you feeling well, *Liebling*?" Mama slipped into German in her anxiety.

Anna did not look up.

"I'm fine," she growled.

"You don't look well, does she, Ernst?" Mama would not let the subject go.

Gretchen, too, looked anxiously at Anna. Was it because of the presents?

"Leave her alone, Klara," Papa said lightly. "She just wants more room for dessert, don't you, Anna?"

Anna slumped so that her face was in shadow.

"That's right," she managed to answer.

After that, she had to eat all her dessert. It was an apple, a Tallman Sweet, her favorite kind. Anna chewed and swallowed, chewed and swallowed. The apple had no taste at all.

As soon as she could get away, she went up and got herself ready for bed.

"Anna, are you asleep so soon?" Mama poked her head in around the curtain Anna had carefully drawn all the way shut.

Anna lay still and kept her eyes closed. She took long, steady breaths. Finally, her mother tiptoed away.

Then Anna opened her eyes. Once more, she would try to think. Surely there was something she could do to make good the words she had flung so proudly and defiantly at the others.

She thought and thought. There must be a way. There had to be.

But when she entered the schoolroom the next morning and banged down in her desk, Anna Solden still had not had a single idea.

And she had given up hoping.

15 • MISS WILLIAMS ASKS

Anna saw the surprise on Miss Williams' face. For a long time now, she, Anna, had come into the room with a smile for her teacher. But she did not feel like smiling. And she did not care what Miss Williams thought about it either.

She opened the lid of her desk, grabbed her pencil box, slammed down the desk lid and put down the pencil box with another crash.

"Good morning, Anna," Miss Williams said evenly.

Anna considered not answering. She glowered at the pencil box and let one second tick past, and then another. But in spite of herself, she looked up and met the teacher's steady gaze.

"Good morning," Anna muttered.

Bernard strolled over and stood beside her.

"What's got into you, kid?" he asked, his voice low, teasing, very kind.

Anna remembered just two days before. Isobel and Ben and she had been talking about the schoolyard bullies who waited for them and called names and threw snowballs. Bernard had overheard and the four of them had planned a counterattack. The two boys had been stunned when, suddenly, four of the victims had come charging after them, armed with snowballs of their own.

"Our aim won't be very good," Bernard had said, "so we'll have to have lots and make a big noise. They're cowards anyway. You'll see."

The bullies had given in almost at once. But the four fighters had chased them a couple of blocks before they had collapsed in the snow and let them go. How they had laughed! How strong Bernard had seemed! A mighty champion like Saint George slaying the dragon!

But even Saint George could not help her now.

"Nothing's got into me," she said sullenly, hating herself because she was lying to Bernard, but not knowing what else to do.

How could she explain about Rudi and what Gretchen had said and how she had boasted? It would all sound stupid. It *was* stupid.

Bernard stayed by her a moment longer, in case she changed her mind. Anna sat still.

Go away, she thought. Just go away.

"All right, Bernard," Miss Williams said. "It's time we got started."

Anna's class was small. They were like a family. Closer than some families. They knew Anna better, cared about her more, in many ways, than Rudi and Gretchen, Frieda and Fritz. As the morning went on and her unhappiness remained, they all felt it.

"Isobel, you have half your arithmetic wrong!" Miss Williams exclaimed.

Isobel was a mathematical genius.

"I'm sorry," Isobel said, flushing. She looked over at Anna, who was staring blindly at her speller. "I just couldn't keep my mind on it," she confessed.

Miss Williams looked at Anna too.

"Miss Williams, may I go and get a drink?" Ben asked suddenly.

"This is your third drink in an hour," the teacher said.

Ben squirmed. "I'm hot," he mumbled.

He did not look at Anna but he might as well have. Miss Williams said quietly, "All right, Benjamin, but come right back."

"My stomach aches," Jane Summers said when it was nearly noon.

Anna was startled out of her own misery. She looked over at Jane, only to find Jane staring back at her, her face screwed up with worry. Anna blinked. Then she decided she was crazy.

"Put your head down on your desk and rest for a

while, Jane," Miss Williams said. "Maybe it'll be better in a minute or two."

A moment later she said, "Bernard, haven't you anything to do?"

Anna glanced up again, in greater surprise. Bernard always worked hard. He was going to be famous when he grew up. He was going to write an encyclopedia. But he was sitting with a pile of spitballs on his desk, right out in the open.

He too gave Anna a sudden look. Then he swept the spitballs out of sight and opened a book. He did not even try to make an excuse.

"I'm reading," he said instead.

Anna watched him out of the corner of her eye. She did not want Bernard to get into trouble. She waited for him to turn a page. He just sat. Minutes passed. The page never turned.

They all went home for lunch. They all came back. Anna's unhappiness returned with her.

Nobody knew how to help. Nobody could guess what was wrong. Everybody waited and watched, waited and grew more and more on edge.

Anna was back at her speller. She had not learned anything before lunch. Now the list of words in front of her still made no sense. Suddenly, hopelessly, she jammed the speller out of sight into her desk. As she did, her fingers brushed against the book Miss Williams had given her. Her own book. Her challenge.

Robert Louis Stevenson would know how I feel,

Anna thought. Probably, when he was small, he often wanted to do things and didn't know how.

She took the book out and opened it to the first poem of all. It was a poem she had not seen before because it was really the dedication and it came ahead of the title page. Also, it was written in a script that was harder to read than the other poems. Maybe she had seen it and decided it was too hard and skipped it. The letters were difficult to make out.

It seemed important, though, to read it now, hard or not. The title was a long name which Anna could not pronounce. She did not bother trying. Only half taking in what she read, she started at the top of the first verse. He was writing it to someone who had lain awake, watching over him. She reached the third line.

For your most comfortable hand
Which led me through the uneven land . . .

That she knew all about. It was the land where Awkward Anna lived and where she did not know what to do. If only there were a comfortable hand she could take! She understood exactly what a comfortable hand must be. "Get comfortable," Miss Williams would say and they would all relax, ready for a record or a story. "Are you comfortable, my little one?" Papa would ask, coming up to tuck in her covers.

Oh, Papa, Papa! Anna thought, needing his help so badly, and yet knowing she could not ask for it.

Then the first tear slid down her nose. The first . . .

and the second . . . and the third. She could not stop them. Anna Elisabeth Solden, who never cried unless she was by herself and sure of being left alone, was crying now in front of a whole roomful of people—and there was not a single thing she could do about it.

Giving up pretending nothing was the matter, Miss Williams fetched a chair and sat down beside the weeping child.

"Tell me about it," she said quietly. "Maybe there's some way I can help."

"There is nothing . . ." choked Anna.

"Yes, Anna, there is something." Miss Williams stayed where she was.

Ben came and stood on Anna's other side. Isobel put down her pencil with a sigh of relief and added her voice to the teacher's.

"Go on and tell her, Anna. Miss Williams will know what you can do. Just tell."

Not daring to hope, Anna started to explain.

From the beginning, everyone listened. When she finished, even the oldest two were nodding in agreement. They, too, wanted a Christmas gift they could give their parents. They, too, with their poor vision, had always been awkward and unskilled.

"If I could only read music . . ." Mavis Jones said wistfully. "The piano teacher gets so mad!"

"My Aunt Mary keeps saying and saying I could learn to knit if I'd just hold my needles the way she does," Josephine Peterson put in. "She tells me to watch—but I can't see what she means, and she can't understand why."

The boys could not use tools the way their fathers did, the way even their brothers did, so easily, so quickly.

Anna was not, after all, the only odd man out. That was what Miss Williams called it—being the odd man out.

Jimmy Short had tried having a paper route. "But I couldn't see the numbers on the houses," he said. "I can't make change fast, either. Nickels and quarters look too much the same."

"None of us can earn money, really," Bernard summed it up, "or make anything good. I want to make one really good thing, just once—and watch their eyes pop!"

"You are a show-off, Bernard," Miss Williams told him. Bernard laughed, not minding. In spite of her teasing, he knew the teacher understood.

All the rest of the day the children could feel her thinking. They were extra good, especially quiet. Nobody raised an unnecessary question. Ben stopped going for drinks from the fountain. Nobody asked to leave the room for any reason.

"Let's make sure I have this clear," Miss Williams said finally. "Perhaps I *can* help but it will take some planning. We'd need money for supplies. . . . You don't want to ask for money at home, am I right?"

Nobody wanted to ask for money.

"It has to be a surprise," Anna said. "The others—Rudi and Gretchen and the twins—will all have surprises."

"Yes, Anna, I know," the teacher said.

"Wait and see," Isobel whispered to Anna. "She'll find a way. Miss Williams can do anything."

But maybe there is no way, thought Anna.

She looked at Isobel's face, bright with faith. She studied Miss Williams' face, deep in thought. Suddenly, it seemed to Anna terribly important to believe. Maybe if she believed hard enough, it would help.

I do believe. There will be a way, Anna whispered under her breath.

Then, all at once, Miss Williams smiled. Her head lifted.

"What is it, Miss Williams?" Ben asked excitedly.

"I think . . . you'll have to wait and see, Ben," the teacher answered.

But everyone knew that it had happened. A way had been found.

16 • ANNA WORKS A MIRACLE

They were going to make wastepaper baskets.

Anna stared uncertainly at the queer collection of things Miss Williams said they were going to need. There were circles and ovals of wood with holes drilled in a neatly spaced row around each edge. There were bundles of straight sticks, cream-colored and clean. There were lengths of reed, rolled up and tied in bunches so they would not spring free and trail all over the room. Some of the reeds were flat and as wide as her finger. Some were round and thin like brittle brown twine.

It looked complicated. It looked much too hard for

her to do by herself. Yet she had to do it on her own. The others were not having help.

Miss Williams did not look worried.

"I wish I had a finished basket to show you," she told the troubled faces grouped around her. "But it will be all right. I promise you."

Anna was comforted. She had never known the teacher to break a promise.

"Miss Williams, where did you get this stuff? Who paid?" asked Bernard, who did understand about the Depression; his father had been without work for three months.

Miss Williams smiled at him and then at Anna.

"A friend of Anna's bought most of the materials," she told the class.

"A friend of Anna's!"

"Boy, Anna, who's your rich friend?"

"I have no such friend," Anna protested. She could not believe Miss Williams would have betrayed her but she had to know. "You didn't tell? It isn't Papa?"

"Not your father," the teacher said quickly. "You have other friends. It was Dr. Schumacher."

"Dr. Schumacher!" Anna breathed.

"Where did he find so much money?" Bernard asked practically.

"Doctors are all rich," Josephine Peterson told him.

"That is not true, Josie," the teacher corrected her. "Now people are having a hard time paying their bills, so they often leave the doctor till last. But Dr. Schumacher has no wife and children of his own to make Christmas for—and Anna is a special friend of his. He told me so himself."

Anna remembered how she had felt that day in his office when the doctor had said she must go to a special class.

He said I would like it and I do, Anna thought. He was my friend even then.

"He didn't do it all," guessed Bernard, studying the supplies. "I'll bet you helped, Miss Williams."

"A little," the teacher admitted, her cheeks flushing under his direct gaze. "I have no family in Toronto either."

"How about your mother and your sisters?" the class wanted to know.

Miss Williams had often told them stories about her childhood. They knew her family well.

"They're in Vancouver." The teacher got busy as she talked, moving books on her desk. "It's too far to go for Christmas but I already have a box full of presents from out West."

The others were distracted by talk of presents. Only Bernard still remained grave and Anna thoughtful.

I could ask Papa to invite them, she told herself. It can't hurt to ask. Miss Williams would like our tree. Dr. Schumacher is busy, but maybe he'd have time that night.

"Now let's begin," Miss Williams said.

Anna was still worried but she watched carefully and listened hard. It did not sound impossible.

First they had to choose the shape they wanted their

baskets to be. Anna picked an oval base. It looked good and big—she did not want to make a small present. She had just learned how to use a ruler. She took hers out of her desk and measured the piece of wood. It was six inches wide at the center and ten inches long. Anna smiled and put the ruler back.

Next they put the reeds to soak in a bucket of water. Anybody could do that. Anna did it carefully, slowly. Josie hurried and broke one of her reeds.

"Treat them gently, Josie," Miss Williams warned. "Watch how Anna handles hers."

By the middle of the afternoon the reeds were pliable enough to weave. Anna put in the upright pegs first. They had to be even. She placed each one slowly, coaxing it, guiding it through the correct hole, measuring first with her eyes and then with her ruler.

"That's it, Isobel. Good, Veronica," Miss Williams went from one to another. "Not so fast, Jimmy. They're uneven at the top."

She paused by Anna's desk. The others were getting ahead of Anna but she was paying no attention to that. She wanted this basket to be just right, like something Gretchen would make, or Mama.

"That's perfect, Anna," the teacher said.

Perfect!

Anna started to tuck in the ends, one behind the other, so that the underside of her basket would be trim and neat. It made an attractive pattern. She stopped to admire it.

"Let me see that," Isobel said, reaching for it. "Oh, I get it. Thanks, Anna."

She handed the basket back and bent her head over her own, undoing her mistake and fixing it. Anna blinked with surprise.

Then, intently, she listened as Miss Williams explained how to do the actual weaving of the reeds. It sounded almost easy. You started with the thin ones. Anna reached for a length of reed. Her hand shook.

Catch the end behind one of the uprights.

She did that. For an instant, she felt all thumbs. The reed slipped loose. Anna bit her lip and began again, more slowly. This time it stayed put. She took a deep breath, gathered her courage, and started to weave.

In and out, in and out. Each time she had to pull the whole long whip-end of reed all the way through. What seemed like yards and yards of it curled and coiled around her. There! She had done it.

Now pull it tight.

Not too tight, Anna reminded herself.

It must fit snugly around the straight sticks, but pulled too hard, it might break. She tugged at it until it felt exactly the way it should. She did not wonder how she was so certain. Her hands knew.

Miss Williams came to her again. There was not a mistake in the child's work. She was concentrating so intently that she was not even aware of the woman who stood watching her.

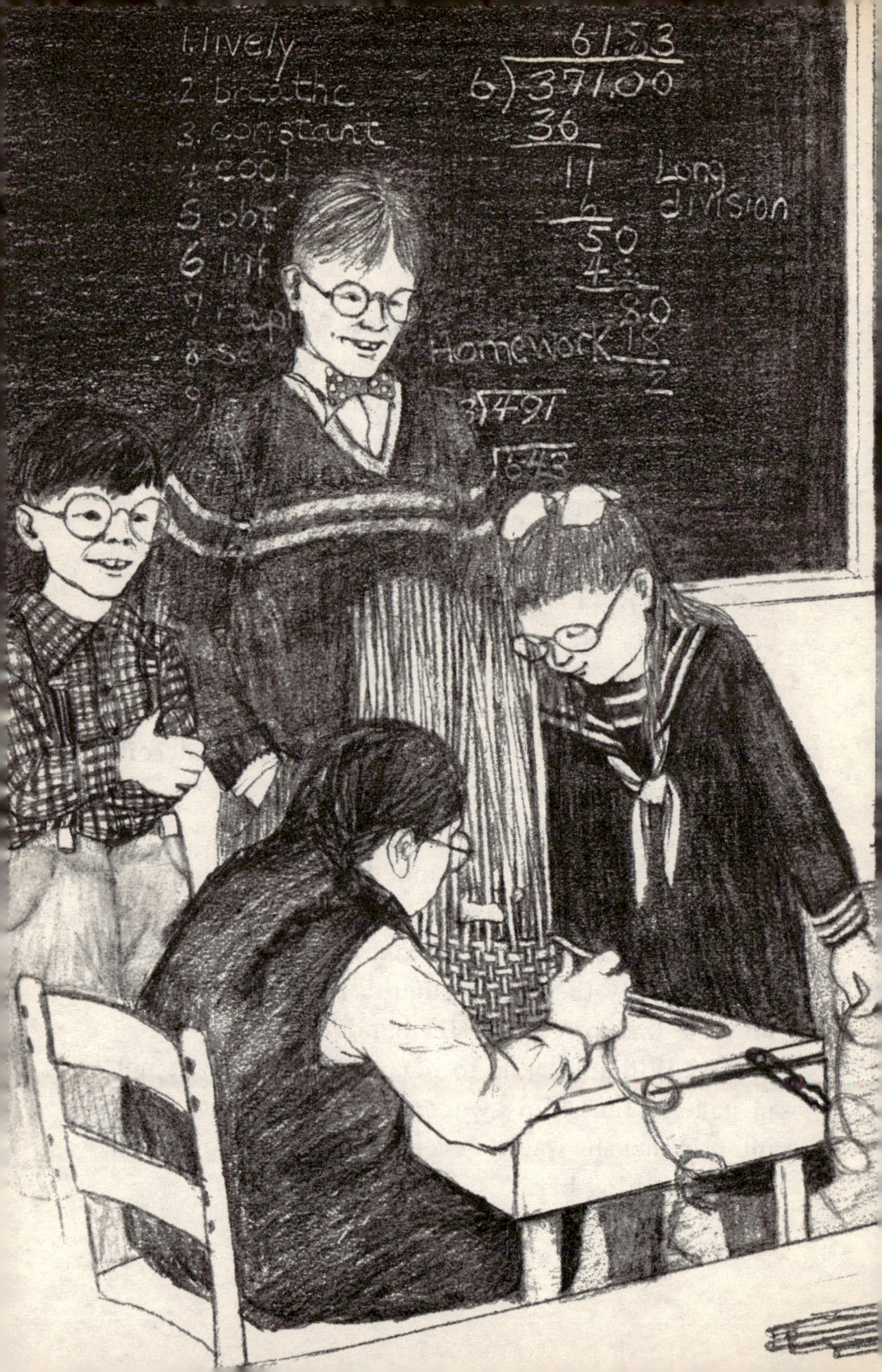
1. lively
2. breathe
3. constant
4. cool
Long division
Homework

"How deft your fingers are, Anna!" Miss Williams said.

Anna's head jerked up. She stared at the teacher. What did "deft" mean?

"Deft means quick and clever," the teacher answered her unspoken question. "Sure of themselves."

Anna knew that up till that very moment, she had had clumsy hands.

"Let me do it, Anna," Mama or Gretchen or even Frieda had often said impatiently. Rudi still called her Awkward Anna when he thought about it.

Now she had deft fingers.

Anna went on weaving the reeds around and around, over and under, over and under. As she worked deftly, neatly, nimbly, a new song was singing itself inside her heart.

A Christmas present,
I am making my Christmas present.
I am making my very own.
It will be from me.

A Christmas present,
A surprise for a Christmas present!
I am making it by myself
And Papa will see.

She had never known such joy. But Miss Williams made them stop long before they were finished.

"There is still something called Spelling," she told them dryly. "And Arithmetic, too, Jimmy."

The next day she gave them time to work on the baskets again, though. Slowly the sides rose. Anna finished with the narrow round reeds and began to weave the flat ones. In and out, in and out.

"My hand's tired," Josie complained. Her basket was messy too.

Anna's hand was not one bit tired. And her basket was not messy.

"She's pretty good for a kid, isn't she?" Bernard said to Miss Williams.

"Not just for a kid," Miss Williams answered. "Anna has a gift for taking infinite pains."

Even Bernard had to have that explained, though he had spoken English all his life.

I wish I could make him a present too, Anna thought. And Isobel and Ben . . . and Miss Williams . . . and Dr. Schumacher.

She could never do it. Not five more presents! She who had not even been able to make one until Miss Williams showed her how. But she thought about it, as her hands pulled the long reeds through and pushed them back. She thought and she began to see how she might.

The basket must be done first though. Her excitement mounted as she neared the end. When she was two inches from the top, she went back to the thin, round reeds. It was like making a border. Then, suddenly, it was complete. It stood almost a foot high. The sides slanted out a little, gracefully. (Several of the others had not been able to manage this. Theirs went straight up like stovepipes.) All the ends were tucked in out of sight. There were no gaps. Anna turned it around slowly, gloating over it.

"Take your pencils and print your initials on the bottom," Miss Williams instructed. "I have arranged to have them painted at the School for the Blind. I wouldn't want you to get them mixed up when they come back."

Anna laughed. As though she would ever confuse her basket with anybody else's! She printed her initials clearly on the white wood.

A. E. S.

Then the baskets were taken away.

At home, the other four were busy with their plans.

Gretchen waited and waited for Papa to offer her the money so she could refuse. Papa seemed to have forgotten.

"You'd better tell him anyway," Rudi decided. "We want them not to worry."

"About the Christmas money, Papa . . ." Gretchen began that night at supper.

Mama interrupted. Her face was very red and she did not look at the children while she talked. She stared at a spot on the table.

"Gretchen, I was meaning to tell you. This year Papa and I would rather not have any presents. Your love, that is enough for us. We . . . Really, that is the way we want it. There will still be the tree, of course. Don't be afraid. But . . ."

"That's fine, Mama," Gretchen managed to break in. "I . . . we . . ."

Rudi kicked her under the table and she was quiet.

"We understand," Rudi told his parents. "Don't worry."

Later, when the children found themselves alone for a moment, he said to the others, "It's even better this way. They won't expect a thing. It will be a complete surprise."

"Three complete surprises," Fritz reminded him with a giggle.

Anna said nothing at all.

As Christmas Eve drew closer and closer, the four older children would not tell each other what they were up to, but hints flew back and forth. Gretchen hid her knitting quick as a wink when Papa or Mama came into the room and she would not let anyone look at it closely. But they all knew it was something blue—and then something yellow.

The twins were shoveling snow after school. Not many people could pay to have snow shoveled, but Frieda and Fritz had kept asking from door to door until they found two or three customers.

Rudi was busy playing hockey.

"Don't worry about me. I have days and days yet," he told them.

"But what are you planning to get?" Fritz plagued him. "Just give us a rough idea. We're getting something Papa will really like, something he doesn't have —and always wanted."

"We hope," Frieda added.

"Mine's going to be something that's a special Christmas thing. . . . You'll see when the time comes. I have to go." Rudi brushed by them and was gone into the winter world of ice and hockey sticks and pucks. He felt completely Canadian.

Anna did not hint. Nobody knew, nobody for one second suspected that she too was working on a Christmas gift. The other four did not think of her at all.

17 • THE DAYS BEFORE CHRISTMAS

One night, Anna went to Papa with her amazing idea.

It's only Papa, she reminded herself as she tried to decide on the right words.

But she had to screw up her courage and the words came out all muddled. Staring down at her father's shoes, Anna almost wished she had not even tried.

"Dr. Schumacher and Miss Williams!" Papa exclaimed. "But . . . but why, Anna?"

"Miss Williams' mother is in Vancouver and Betty and Joan are too. They're her sisters," Anna explained in a rush. "But Miss Williams cannot go to see them because there's no money this year."

Papa nodded. That much he understood.

"And Miss Williams said Dr. Schumacher has no wife or children. Maybe he does have a mother, though . . ." Anna stopped at this new, startling thought.

"No," Papa said. "Franz has no family. He was raised in an orphanage in Berlin."

Anna lifted her head at that. Eagerness lighted her face. "Then he might want to come," she cried. "They both might."

Her father rubbed his chin. His answer came slowly. "Anna, my darling, you know we ourselves will not have such a large Christmas. There will be no wonderful presents. No skates, I'm afraid."

Anna hurried to comfort him. "Gretchen already knows. Don't worry, Papa," she said.

"Does she?" Papa sighed. Then he looked thoughtful again. Reaching out, he held her by both shoulders. "About these people coming though, Anna . . ."

"It isn't only the presents," Anna said.

Yet, if Papa did not understand, she knew no way to make it clear. She twisted free and ran for the door.

"All right. I will ask," her father called after her.

She did not turn. He did not know whether she had heard.

Anna had not heard, but by the next morning, she was too busy to brood over it any longer. She was making and finding other gifts. She began with Isobel's.

It was hard to get it done without Isobel looking over

her shoulder and asking questions. At last Anna went to the teacher and asked if she could stay in at recess to work on it.

"May I see it when it is done?" Miss Williams asked.

"It is a funny present," Anna said very seriously. "It is . . . how do you say it? . . . a joke."

"A joke!"

Anna nodded, still not smiling. "I will let you see," she promised.

She made Isobel a dictionary. On each page was a word Isobel had taught Anna during the months they had known each other. Above the words were pictures.

When she took it shyly to Miss Williams, the teacher laughed aloud.

"Oh Anna, I knew you had imagination but I never dreamed you had such a sense of humor," she said.

She was looking at the page which said "Undertaker." The picture showed a coffin. Anna herself was sitting bolt upright in it. She was calling, "Help!" Her braids stuck straight up in the air with horror and her eyes, behind her glasses, were perfectly round. Isobel, ringlets and all, was the undertaker, spade in hand. There was another picture of Isobel as a lamplighter, falling off her ladder. There was one of Halloween, with a ghost chasing Isobel, who dashed madly across the page. All the pictures were full of action and fun. Isobel starred in each one.

Anna wrote a poem for Ben. She had a feeling it was not a terribly good poem, not like Robert Louis Stevenson's. But it said what she felt. She lettered it carefully on a Christmas card she made out of construction paper.

> Benjamin Nathaniel
> Is as brave as Daniel.
> When snowballs fly
> Through the sky,
> When big boys came
> And yelled a bad name,
> Ben does not run away.
> He says we must stay.
> He gets Bernard to come
> And we all help some.
> Then the big boys are made
> Very afraid.
> We get them to run
> But Ben is the one
> Who tells us to stay
> And not run away.
> Benjamin Nathaniel
> Is braver than Daniel.
> We stand by his side
> With pride.

Smiling, she hid it away in her desk.

What could she do for Bernard, though? She knew she could not write another poem. Ben's had taken her days.

Then, like a miracle, she found a dime on the sidewalk. She could buy Bernard a present—and she knew exactly what he would like: rubber bands for shooting spitballs! She got them at the store from Papa.

"What do you want them for?" Papa asked.

"It is a secret," said Anna.

Papa looked at the dime in her hand.

"There was nobody near who could have dropped it. I looked," she assured him.

"You buy ice cream and I could just let you have the rubber bands," Papa offered. The Soldens did not sell ice cream.

Anna shook her head.

"I want to pay for them, Papa," she insisted.

Her father gave her the elastics. She hurried away before Mama got curious too.

Now she had something for everyone but Miss Williams and the doctor. Once again it was like a miracle. A package arrived from Aunt Tania in Frankfurt. Mama handed out pieces of marzipan. Anna got two. The other children gobbled theirs up at once. Anna put hers carefully away. All her gifts were ready.

Dr. Schumacher himself delivered the baskets back to the classroom.

"I couldn't carry them all at once, Eileen," he said. "I'll fetch the rest."

Isobel nudged Anna.

"What is it?" Anna whispered, staring not at Isobel but at the heap of baskets on the teacher's desk.

"He called her Eileen!"

"Did he?" Anna said, still paying no attention.

Now Miss Williams was handing out the baskets

one by one. They were beautiful beyond belief. Had something happened to hers?

"And here's Anna's," Miss Williams said.

She placed it on the girl's desk. Anna made no move to touch it. She simply stared. It was dark green now, with tiny threads of gold running through it. It was the most splendid thing, the most incredibly perfect present she had ever seen.

She looked down at her own two hands in wonder. They looked just as usual. Her fingernails were dirty. Could those hands actually have made this basket?

With intense care, she picked it up and looked. There, on the bottom, in her very own printing, it said "A. E. S."

School was over. The other children bundled into their coats, clutched their baskets, and headed for home.

"Coming, Anna?" Isobel asked.

"Not right now," Anna said. "You go ahead."

She sat at her desk and waited. Dr. Schumacher was still there too. He and Miss Williams laughed together.

"I told you she was in love," Isobel whispered and, shrugging at Anna's blank face, she too departed.

The teacher noticed Anna a moment later.

"Oh, Anna, I thought you went with the others," she said. "Was there something you wanted?"

"May I leave my basket here till the last day?" Anna asked.

Miss Williams glanced at the doctor, who stood listening. Then she turned back to Anna.

"Of course you may," she said gently.

She did not ask why. She knew that Anna still kept her beloved book of Stevenson's poems in her desk. She had not even taken it home overnight.

"How are the glasses working?" Franz Schumacher asked.

Anna looked up at him through them. She wished she had words to tell him what he had done for her.

"They are very good, thank you," she said primly.

"I remember when I first got my glasses," Dr. Schumacher said. "What an exciting place the world was, all at once! So full of things I had not dreamed were there! . . . Would you like a ride home, Miss Solden?"

He knows about the glasses without me telling, Anna thought. He knows how glad I am.

She was not sure about taking the ride, though. Mama was so fussy about them taking rides. Then she looked at Dr. Schumacher again.

"I would like a ride," she said.

"How about you, Eileen?" he asked then.

"No. I'll be awhile yet," she said. "Thank you anyway."

"I'll see you at eight, then," Dr. Schumacher said.

Anna, putting on her coat, almost missed those last words. Then everything Isobel had said fell into place.

Miss Williams and the doctor—in love!!

Anna was glad Isobel had gone. She would not have known what to say to her. The whole idea would take getting used to.

The girl and the man drove along in a comfortable silence. He did not pester her with the usual grown-up questions.

"That basket of yours is beautiful work, Anna," he said once. "You can be very proud of it."

"Yes," said Anna simply. "I am."

But when she got out of the car, she did remember to thank him. She even invited him in, although her parents would not be home yet. Mama always invited people in. At least, she had in Frankfurt.

"Another time, little one," he said with a smile.

Anna walked into the house humming to herself. He had called her "little one" the way Papa did. And, long ago, he had said she was "as light as a feather" and "a challenge."

His hair is gray, though. He is too old for Miss Williams, Anna decided.

Then the image of her lovely basket rose before her, and, forgetting the doctor and her teacher, she went slowly up the stairs, hugging close to herself her Christmas secret. Somehow she must manage not to tell.

The time passed like a turtle dawdling. But bit by bit, it did go by. At last it was the final day of school, the day before Christmas Eve.

That night Anna carried her basket home clasped in her arms as tenderly as if it were a newborn baby.

As she walked, she thought of how Isobel had laughed till tears ran down her cheeks when she went through her dictionary. Ben had been struck speechless by his poem.

"May I put it on the bulletin board?" Miss Williams asked.

Both Ben and Anna blushed. Ben nodded.

"The kid's a genius," Bernard said proudly, as though it were his doing.

Then she had produced his rubber bands.

"Oh, Anna!" Miss Williams had gasped, laughing almost as hard as Isobel had a few moments before. "Don't you have any respect for my peace of mind?"

Anna had shaken her head. Both her dimples had showed.

"Watch it, kid," Bernard had warned. "You're getting as fresh as a Canadian."

"I am a Canadian," Anna told him.

She had left the piece of marzipan on Miss Williams' desk when the teacher was out of the room for a moment. The teacher had not discovered it before Anna left. She was glad. It was such a small bit of candy.

She still had Dr. Schumacher's at home. Maybe Papa would help her to deliver it—maybe they could drop it into his letter box.

She was nearly home. She hugged the basket more closely and kept an eye out for her brothers and sisters. There was Frieda, shoveling the Blairs' walk. Anna breathed quickly. But she got safely by. Frieda did not look up.

The others were busy when she entered the house.

Nobody paid any attention as she walked across the hall and up to her alcove. She tried hard to walk as usual. Her feet kept wanting to leap and skip. When the curtain was drawn, she knelt and hid the precious basket away under her cot.

Excitement bubbled and boiled inside her when she went back downstairs but she went on walking sedately. She had kept this secret for weeks. She could get through one more day.

Rudi was out late that night. Gretchen was shut in her room, knitting frantically. The twins whispered together. Mama and Papa looked tired but happier than they had been. Anna watched everyone and waited for the hours to pass. She counted the hours.

A full twenty-four, at least!

Her parents would have to work the next day even though it was the day before Christmas. They might even be late. They would probably not have the tree ready till at least eight o'clock. Maybe nine even!

Now Mama was looking through Christmas tree decorations they had brought from Frankfurt. Some were broken. Was the angel broken? No—there she was in Mama's hand.

All at once, Anna could stay there no longer. Without a word to anyone, she got up and went up to bed. If she had not escaped and lain still, her face turned to the wall, she was certain the magnificent truth would have burst from her.

One more day, she chanted. One more day!

But the clock chimed eleven before she fell asleep.

18 • CHRISTMAS EVE

The next night, as soon as Papa had his coat off, the five children were sent out for a walk.

"As if we don't know what they're doing," Rudi scoffed.

He had only just come in. His cheeks were still red from the wind.

"You like it as much as we do, Rudi, so don't pretend you don't," Gretchen said.

Rudi did not answer, but Anna knew Gretchen was right.

"Can't we go home *now*?" Fritz begged for the hundredth time.

His big brother consulted their father's watch, which

had been loaned to him for this exact reason.

"Fifteen minutes longer," he said.

"Fifteen!" Fritz wailed.

It sounded like eternity.

Anna thought fleetingly of what Isobel had told her. Isobel had helped choose her family's tree and had joined in trimming it. The Browns would not celebrate Christmas till tomorrow morning. There would be no candles, only colored lights. Isobel had thought Anna's way was "queer"—but Anna felt no envy.

Poor Isobel, she thought instead.

Then, suddenly it was time. They ran up the walk, bumping into each other in their hurry. They got out of their coats. All eyes were on the door to the living room, tightly closed. Even Rudi forgot about being oldest.

"Ready, Mama?" Papa asked.

"Ready," Mama said, behind the door.

Papa threw it open—and there, before their dazzled eyes, stood the Christmas tree!

Anna could not have described it, although she saw every detail: the glass balls, the tiny candles blazing. There were candy ornaments too, circlets of spun sugar, chocolate balls done up in silver paper. At the very top, the small angel perched, her gauzy wings catching the light.

The Soldens marched in singing. There was no English now, no thought of it. The song about the Christmas tree had to be in the language of the country from which it had come, long ago.

O Tannenbaum, o Tannenbaum,
Wie grün sind deine Blätter!

As they sang, Anna felt she might burst with joy.

Next Papa read the Christmas story and prayed. Then he was handing out presents. Anna had expected maybe one present or two. But no! Soon she held a pair of cherry red mittens Mama had made for her without her ever knowing.

She must have done them late, after I was in bed, Anna thought. She knew how tired her mother was at nights. She swallowed and hugged the mittens to her.

There was a game too. Snakes and Ladders, it was called. Anna opened it up and looked. With her glasses, it was easy to see. It wouldn't be like the old days when nobody wanted her to play. She would show them what she could do with this game of her own.

"Thank you, Papa," she said. "Mama, thank you."

"Something else for Miss Anna Elisabeth Solden," Papa said.

It wasn't a doll with curly hair and eyes that opened and shut. That was what Isobel wanted. It was something which pleased Anna even more.

"A book!" she breathed.

It was called *Now We Are Six*. Papa had written inside the front.

"For my Anna, who loves to read poems, with love from Papa."

How had he known? Oh, of course he knew about her loving poems! He had taught her many by heart.

But that she could read a book by herself? An English book! She raised wondering eyes to him. He caught her look and smiled.

"Miss Williams and I had a talk," he said simply.

Anna blushed. She would bring home *A Child's Garden of Verses* right after Christmas. She should have done it before.

Throughout the excitement of opening their presents, though, all five children were preoccupied, thinking more of the gifts they had to give than of those they were getting.

How amazed Papa and Mama were going to be! Stunned!

"How about some carols," Mama suggested.

Rudi held up his hand like a young king.

"No. Wait," he commanded. He turned to Gretchen, his blue eyes blazing. "You first, Gretel," he said.

Gretchen had her things hidden under the couch cushions. "Papa, Anna, get up!" she ordered.

She had made each of her parents a scarf. A soft yellow one for Mama, a bright blue one for Papa.

"The color of your eyes," Gretchen said to Papa.

Mama's had a special lacy pattern which had kept Gretchen busy counting stitches for days.

"Lovely, Gretel. So beautiful," Mama said proudly. "But I told you . . ."

"I know," the girl told her, "but we all have something, all but Anna, of course."

Anna tensed but remained silent.

Mama was draping her scarf around her neck. It set off her dark hair beautifully. Gretchen glowed. She sent a sidelong look at Rudi. Beat that if you can, it said.

"Twins," Rudi directed.

"Our present is for Papa," Fritz apologized to his mother.

Fritz and Frieda had wrapped up the parcel in special paper they had made.

"Like Canadians," Fritz explained.

Papa opened the package carefully. Inside was a pipe and, with it, pipe tobacco, a tobacco pouch, pipe cleaners and matches. The twins had started shopping, sure they had a fortune to spend, but by the time they had bought their father everything they thought he would need, their funds had vanished.

"Perhaps you could smoke it too, Mama?" Frieda suggested.

"Maybe . . . maybe," Mama nodded solemnly.

They all burst out laughing then, the twins laughing hardest of all.

Papa had difficulty getting his pipe started. He had never smoked a pipe before, he admitted. The entire family watched with interest. Anna sat on her hands and fought to keep herself from dashing up for the basket. It should be last, she was certain. She was the youngest.

Papa puffed thoughtfully. Then he coughed.

"A fine pipe, twins," he wheezed, wiping away tears.

Tears of joy, Frieda told herself happily.

"A truly magnificent present," Papa went on, holding the pipe away from himself and regarding it with respect.

Rudi left the room then. The rest waited eagerly. Although their brother had walked out so calmly, they knew he was terribly excited. His present was sure to be something extraordinary.

He returned carrying a tall, scraggly poinsettia. Without a word, he held it out to his mother. Mama held the chipped pot on her knee and gazed up at the red flower which came just above her eyes.

"Rudi, a real Christmas flower," she gasped, her dark eyes wide. "How did you get this? We never had anything prettier, even at home in Frankfurt, did we, Ernst?"

Rudi reddened. Slowly at first, and then all in a rush, he made his confession.

"I meant to get something a long time ago, but I didn't even notice the days going. They needed me at the rink because I'm the fastest skater really. When I went to try to get work, all the snow had all been shoveled. I thought I could be a delivery boy but everywhere I asked, they said no. You had to have a bicycle."

The family sat listening silently as his words stumbled on. This was so unlike Rudi, always proud and right. He gave them no chance to interrupt. He wanted to get it over with. He was past the worst part now. He put his hands in his pockets and relaxed.

"Then I went to Mr. Simmons' flower shop. It was

. . . last night. I was sure there would be nothing. But he's nice at church and I've seen him in your store, Papa. And he said, 'Are you Ernst Solden's boy?' I told him yes, and how I'd tried for a job but couldn't find one. I didn't beg, though, Papa."

"I know that, Rudi," Papa said. They all knew that.

"Well, he said if I wanted to take a couple of last-minute orders to people who live near here, he'd give me a plant nobody had bought. That's why I was late getting home last night. I was working," Rudi ended proudly, as pleased with himself as ever.

"It is beautiful, Rudi, and you were a brave boy to keep trying that way," Mama said warmly.

"Papa, don't you like your pipe?" Fritz asked anxiously. Papa had let it go out.

"I do. I do indeed!" Ernst Solden said, picking it up and holding it as though it were precious. "It takes getting used to, that is all, Fritz. Right now, I cannot pay attention to everything else and smoke my new pipe properly all at the same time."

Fritz smiled with relief. Rudi frowned at having his moment of triumph interrupted. He wondered suddenly if Papa really *did* like the twins' present. That pipe tobacco had a strange smell. Rudi tried to breathe shallowly.

Mama was still lost in admiration of the poinsettia.

"I do not know where to put this," she hesitated, touching the red leaves lovingly. "Perhaps on the mantel . . ."

She got up and tried the flower there, setting it right

in the center in the position of honor. Papa had to hold the plant for her while she actually moved the chiming clock to one side. When the flower was centered, she stepped back and studied it. Everybody else studied it too. It was important that it be right. It was right—exactly.

"Perfect," Mama said, turning to face her family.

In that moment, Anna was gone. She who always walked heavily, uncertain of where her feet would land, now slipped from the room without a sound.

"Anna . . ." Mama started to call after her. Ernst Solden put out his hand quickly and touched her arm.

"No, Klara. Wait. She'll be right back," he said.

The others had not even seen Anna go. They were telling each other all over again about their adventures getting the gifts: how Mama had nearly caught Gretchen knitting more than once, what trouble the twins had had deciding which pipe to choose, the places Rudi had had to deliver flowers.

Mama put her hands over her ears.

"Oh, it is good Christmas is not every day!" she cried. "I am nearly deaf."

But she was still worried about Anna. Whatever Ernst said, maybe she should go and see. The little one should not be left out.

And then, there stood Anna herself with the waste-paper basket.

19 • FROM ANNA

It was not wrapped. But Anna had stopped at Papa's desk and found a piece of plain paper. On it she had printed briefly, in large letters,

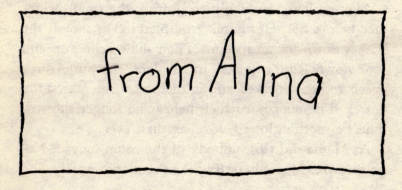

from Anna

The letters wobbled and were uneven because, despite her care, she could not keep her hand from shaking. She had folded the paper and hung it over the edge of the basket. Now she simply thrust the whole thing at her mother and said in a voice which was almost defiant, "There. I made it at school."

Mama stared at the basket and then at the child who had pushed it into her hands. Her eyes were disbelieving. Her mouth opened but no words came out. Papa, who had sat down, started to get up again. Then he smiled a slow smile and sank back in his chair. This time, it was up to Klara.

At last Mama's voice returned.

"Anna! Oh, *mein Liebling,* how . . . how wonderful! I cannot . . . Ernst, look! Do you see? Anna has given us a basket. You did not make this, Anna, your own self?"

"Yes, I did," Anna said, standing straight. She felt like a giant, like a soaring bird, like a Christmas tree with every candle alight.

Mama turned suddenly away from the small bright face before her. Her hands trembled too as she set the basket down for an instant. Then she reached up and took down Rudi's flower. In its place, she put Anna's green and gold basket, and in the basket she placed the flower. The poor pot which held it no longer showed. The poinsettia glowed, lovelier than ever.

As Mama did this, nobody in the room moved. Nobody spoke. Mama herself broke the silence finally. She

stood, looking up at basket and flower, and she said in a choked voice, "I was the blind one all this time. Dr. Schumacher should have given me the glasses."

The words made no sense to Anna. Mama had perfect eyesight. The other four children were also bewildered. But Papa said quickly, "It has not been only you, Klara. We have all failed to see."

Before anyone could figure this out, Mama whirled around and caught Anna to her so swiftly that the girl had no time to dodge. She hugged her small daughter close.

"Tonight . . . tonight you are the dearest, dearest child," Mama said.

She knew Anna would hate to be cried over but she could not help it, and after all, it did not matter. She went on hugging Anna harder than ever, trying to put into the embrace all the other times when Anna had needed to be held and had been hurt instead.

Anna squirmed.

So this was how it was! All this glow and warmth inside and around you, and yet a wrongness there too, because the others were being left out.

Rudi won't like his flower to be in my basket, she thought.

She remembered Gretchen offering to knit something from her, Anna. Suddenly she was sure Gretchen had meant to be kind.

And the twins . . . how must they feel? They had given Mama nothing.

"Don't, Mama," Anna mumbled, pulling to get free.

Rudi spoke then, his voice loud and hard.

"She must have had help," he said.

Right away, the two older girls nodded.

"Anna didn't make that herself," Fritz backed up his brother. "She couldn't."

Papa was on his feet with frightening abruptness. He towered over them, taller than they had ever seen him.

But Anna spoke first. "You are right. I did. I had help," she admitted.

She stood apart from Mama now and faced her brothers and sisters. Her voice, which had been high and clear with excitement moments before, had dulled, grown almost hoarse. But she went on, explaining how the miracle had happened.

"Miss Williams started us off and showed us how. Dr. Schumacher bought the reeds and things. Some other people painted them for us."

Her chin lifted then.

"I did weave it though, all by myself," she said.

Papa ignored her completely. He started with Rudi.

"How could you have brought home this plant without the help of Mr. Simmons, Rudolf?" he asked.

Rudi had no answer. If he had, he would not have dared to speak. Papa's voice was terribly quiet but the words stabbed, each one a dagger thrust. He had called him Rudolf, too. That only happened when he was in serious trouble.

Papa waited, just in case. His son Rudolf seemed to have stopped breathing. Ernst Solden turned from him.

Gretchen knew she came next. She stared at the shabby carpet and wished she were somewhere else. Anywhere! She tried not to think of how Anna had looked standing up in front of them all.

"And were you born knowing how to knit, Gretchen?" her father inquired coldly. "Who loaned you the pattern book? Where did you get the wool?"

The others had not thought of that. Wool did cost money. Had Gretchen earned some? They darted little questioning looks at her but she went on staring at the floor. She knew, and Papa knew, that she had gone to him for that money and that she had sneaked away one of Mama's knitting books. She had to have wool though. How could she have made anything without wool?

Papa did not even wait this time.

"Fritz, Frieda, we have no snow shovel. Yet you had two to work with. I thought the neighbors loaned them to you but they came from the air, did they?"

The twins sat side by side on the couch.

This can't be happening on Christmas Eve, Frieda sobbed inside herself, to Fritz.

Fritz, without saying a word aloud, answered her bleakly, This will be the worst Christmas of our lives.

When Papa had started, Mama had reached out for Anna and pulled her down into a big chair by her side.

It was as though she knew Anna's knees had turned to jelly. Now, though, without letting go her hold on her youngest, she burst into angry speech. And she, too, was on Papa's side against them! It was at the poor twins she glared, missing their misery, seeing only how white Anna had looked before she got her to sit down.

"Your poor Papa was tired and cold but often . . . Do you remember, Fritz? Frieda, have you forgotten so soon—he stopped to help you with that snow while I went in to get supper. Maybe I am imagining things?"

Nobody said she was imagining anything. They all knew she was going to cry again. One more minute and they would all be crying!

Then Papa laughed instead. It croaked oddly, that laugh, but it was real. Still they did not dare to believe.

"What are we doing?" Ernst Solden asked, the harshness gone as quickly as it had come. "Such trouble, such long faces on Christmas Eve. This will never do. All because Anna has given us a present. We should be singing."

He drew Anna up out of her mother's sheltering arms and stood her in front of him.

"Come, Anna, be happy," he told her. "Every one of us would have been proud to make this basket. We can all use it—for years and years! And every one of us is proud of you, even if you did have help, because you did this thing with love and for Christmas. How did you keep such a secret for so long?"

Anna swallowed hard, blinked back the tears that

were stinging her eyes, and fighting to sound like her ordinary self, said, "I kept it at school till yesterday—and then under my bed."

All at once, Gretchen was standing up too. She forgot the awful unhappiness. She pushed close to Papa and grabbed Anna by the arm.

"It is wonderful, Anna, your basket," she blurted. "You never hinted. Not even once!"

The ice was gone from their hearts, from the bright room.

Frieda and Fritz talked together, their words tumbling over each other.

"It is lovely . . ."

"Could you teach me how. . . ?"

"Nobody guessed. *Nobody!*"

"Nobody guessed about your presents either," Anna muttered, shyness and delight washing over her.

But Rudi still had not said anything. It was just a dumb basket. His flower was still the best.

Looking away from the flower, because he could not help seeing the basket too, he caught his mother watching him.

Rudi coughed. Then to his own surprise he found himself standing.

"I don't see how you did it, Anna," he said with complete honesty. "You're just a little kid."

Now they were all laughing all together at the surprise in his voice. Even Mama, still seated in the big chair, joined in. But her glance at Rudi made him feel taller, beloved again, almost his old self.

Frieda spoke plaintively, breaking the last bit of tension.

"Mama, I'm hungry," she announced.

So were the rest and they turned to their mother expectantly. They knew she had a feast ready. She had been baking every evening for the past week and, that very afternoon, she had come home from work early, shutting even Gretchen out of the kitchen while she put on the last finishing touches.

Mama stayed where she was. Her dark eyes twinkled at them.

"Not yet," she said.

"But, Mama . . ."

"Anna's guests are still not here," Klara Solden said calmly.

20 • ONE MORE SURPRISE

"Anna's guests!"

Rudi, Gretchen, Frieda and Fritz stared at their mother. Anna tipped her face up and peered at her father through her moons of glasses.

"Oh, Papa, you asked them!" she cried.

"Yes, I asked them," Papa smiled.

How excited she was! He had never seen her like this, her cheeks so pink, her eyes shining. One of her braids was undone and her glasses were crooked. But her dimples! Had she always had dimples like that?

She's beautiful, her father thought.

"We must wait," he said, "but they'll be here. Franz

is bringing her in his car." There was something in Papa's voice.

Isobel's right, Anna thought. They *are* in love. Her smile grew even wider.

"Let me go, Papa," she said suddenly, "I want to look at my new things while we're waiting."

The others were still exclaiming over the fact that Anna had guests coming, but she could not stand being the center of attention another moment. She went down on her knees beside the tree and picked up *Now We Are Six*. She opened it and held it close to her nose. Good. It smelled all right. The smell of a book was important when you had to hold it so close.

And she had a game, too, and the mittens. She pulled on the mittens and snuggled her hands up against her cheeks.

The doorbell rang.

"There they are, Anna," Papa said. "You go and let them in."

She scrambled up from the floor and, snatching off her mittens, grabbed at her father.

"You come too," she entreated. "I can't by myself."

Mama, worrying about what there was to eat, looked at her impatiently.

"Don't be foolish," she urged, her voice sharpening just a little. "You are keeping them waiting."

"It's all right, Klara. They won't mind a small thing like that," laughed Papa.

He looked down into his daughter's panic-stricken

face. Gently, very gently, he teased, "I thought you were my independent child, my Anna who goes her own way," he said. "You don't need a hand to hold. Not you!"

He was laughing at her. Her own Papa who never laughed at her!

But now Bernard laughed at her every day. Isobel was always laughing at her.

"You *are* funny, Anna," Isobel often said.

Even Miss Williams teased.

And Anna did not mind. Not any more.

"Please, please, Papa," she cried, tugging at his sleeve, even smiling herself, but still wanting him.

"Come on then," he said and gave her his broad hand.

Holding on, she felt her courage return. She walked proudly. She, Anna, had guests.

Not watching where she stepped, she stumbled over a wrinkle in the rug. She would have fallen if Papa had not kept hold of her.

"There goes Awkward Anna!" Fritz laughed.

She turned to glare but the doorbell rang again.

"He said it for fun only," Papa told her, tightening his grip on her hand.

Anna's dimples showed unexpectedly.

"Hurry, Papa," she begged, as though Fritz did not exist.

Together they opened the door to Miss Williams and the doctor.

"Merry Christmas, Anna."

"Merry Christmas, Miss Williams!"

"Oh, it's snowing! Look, *Liebling*, like stars!"

"*Fröhliche Weihnachten*, Franz."

They were inside. The door was shut against the cold and the snow. Anna took her teacher's heavy coat and staggered to the closet with it.

The others had come into the hall now, too. Greetings flew. Then Mama spoke out over them all.

"All right, Frieda. Now we may eat," she said.

They started to follow her, everyone laughing at Frieda's red face.

Questions came at Anna thick and fast.

"Did they like the basket, Anna?" Miss Williams asked.

"Did you surprise them? Did you keep it a secret?" said the doctor.

Before she could begin to answer, the teacher added, "And your tree, Anna! Is it as beautiful as you told us it would be? So lovely you would not even try to draw a picture of it?"

"*Ja*," Anna said. "*Ja, ja, ja!*"

They could not eat now! She must make Mama understand. They must go in and see the tree first. And there was something else, something she had planned to say for a long time but had kept putting off or forgetting.

Only I didn't really, Anna admitted to herself. I was just afraid.

She was not afraid now. But first she must get Mama to listen.

"Mama, Mama, stop. Wait!" she called out, as her mother went to open the dining-room door.

Klara Solden turned. What now? Her mouth went tight. Then she remembered what she had learned that evening.

"What is it, Anna?" she asked.

"We must go to the tree first for just one moment," said Anna.

Her mother hesitated.

But Papa nodded. "She is right, Klara," he said.

Mama let go of the doorknob and came with them. They were standing in front of the tree. It glowed. It was as beautiful as it had been in the very first moment when Papa had let them in to see it. Miss Williams' eyes were wide with wonder.

"I've never seen a tree lit with candles before," she breathed. "Oh, it is lovely."

Anna had known she would like it. It was important that she see it before anything else.

But now, now it was time for the other.

"Maybe later would be better," a voice inside her whispered. "Maybe you should wait until there aren't so many people."

Anna had listened to that voice before. Now she shut her mind to it.

"Mama," she said quickly, while she was still brave, "I have to tell you something."

"Not another surprise," Mama said.

She was still concerned about the food, although really she did know she had more than enough. Yet Dr. Schumacher might be a terribly hungry man!

She looked down and caught Anna waiting for her to listen properly. Oh, she must find time for Anna. From now on, she must always try to find time.

"Yes, Anna," she said, really listening.

"I can speak English," Anna announced.

She giggled then, because the words had come out not in English but in German. Mama would not know what to think. Anna tried again, this time switching to her new language.

"I can speak English, Mama. Not just a little bit. Really. I do it all the time at school. I even think in English now mostly. I do it . . . almost as well as you do."

She knew her English was better than Mama's, but she loved Mama so much tonight.

"English!" Mama said in amazement, forgetting the food entirely. "But at home you speak German only. Day after day!"

"She certainly speaks English at school," Miss Williams said. "She's becoming quite a chatterbox. Isobel is leading her astray."

"Are you surprised, Mama?" Anna persisted. "Are you happy?"

Klara Solden did not know herself how she felt. Her smile did not waver, but there was sadness, too, on her face, for an instant.

"I have no German child left," she said.

"They are all your children," Papa told her, putting his arm around her. "They are Canadian children maybe, but they are all yours, *meine Liebe*. Yes, Anna, she *is* surprised, and she is happy too."

"Mama, listen," Anna rushed on, paying no attention to Papa for once in her life. "Listen to what I have learned for you."

She stood up straight, her feet set a little apart, her hands clasped behind her, her head high. Above her, her perfect basket stood on the mantel, holding Rudi's flower. Taking a deep breath, she began to sing:

"Silent night, holy night,"

"Ach, 'Stille Nacht'!" Mama breathed. She was near tears again but only for a moment.

Anna sang on in English:

"All is calm, All is bright"

Gretchen joined her then, their two voices blending:

"Round yon Virgin mother and child,"

The other three children came in together on the next line:

"Holy infant so tender and mild"

Then the adults sang too, Miss Williams very softly in English, Dr. Schumacher, Papa and Mama in the language in which the words were first written:

"Schlaf in himmlischer Ruh,"
"Sleep in heavenly peace."

Anna led them on into the next verse. You could tell that she was seeing the shepherds, was dazzled by the angels.

She *is* special, my Anna, Papa thought, watching her joyous face. I was right about her all along.

But Anna did not think of such things. She did not remember being Awkward Anna. She did not tell herself she was Miss Williams' "challenge." She did not even hug to her heart that moment when, finally, she had become Mama's "dearest, dearest child."

In her heart it was Christmas, and she was busy singing.